THE PERFECT STRANGER

CHARLOTTE BYRD

CHARLOTTE BYRD
dangerously addictive

Visit my website at www.charlotte-byrd.com

PRAISE FOR CHARLOTTE BYRD

"BEST AUTHOR YET! Charlotte has done it again! There is a reason she is an amazing author and she continues to prove it! I was definitely not disappointed in this series!!" ★★★★★

"LOVE!!! I loved this book and the whole series!!! I just wish it didn't have to end. I am definitely a fan for life!!! ★★★★★

"Extremely captivating, sexy, steamy, intriguing, and intense!" ★★★★★

"Addictive and impossible to put down."
★★★★★

"What a magnificent story from the 1st book through book 6 it never slowed down always surprising the reader in one way or the other. Nicholas and Olive's paths crossed in a most unorthodox way and that's how their story begins it's exhilarating with that nail biting suspense that keeps you riding on the edge the whole series. You'll love it!" ★★★★★

"What is Love Worth. This is a great epic ending to this series. Nicholas and Olive have a deep connection and the mystery surrounding the deaths of the people he is accused of murdering is to be read. Olive is one strong woman with deep convictions. The twists, angst, confusion is all put together to make this worthwhile read."
★★★★★

"Fast-paced romantic suspense filled with twists and turns, danger, betrayal, and so much more." ★★★★★

"Decadent, delicious, & dangerously addictive!" - Amazon Review ★★★★★

"Titillation so masterfully woven, no reader can resist its pull. A MUST-BUY!" - Bobbi Koe, Amazon Review ★★★★★

"Captivating!" - Crystal Jones, Amazon Review ★★★★★

"Sexy, secretive, pulsating chemistry…" - Mrs. K, Amazon Reviewer ★★★★★

"Charlotte Byrd is a brilliant writer. I've read loads and I've laughed and cried. She writes a balanced book with brilliant characters. Well done!" -Amazon Review ★★★★★

"Hot, steamy, and a great storyline." - Christine Reese ★★★★★

"My oh my….Charlotte has made me a fan for life." - JJ, Amazon Reviewer ★★★★★

"Wow. Just wow. Charlotte Byrd leaves me speechless and humble… It definitely kept me on the edge of my seat. Once you pick it up, you won't put it down." - Amazon Review ★★★★★

" Intrigue, lust, and great characters...what more could you ask for?!" - Dragonfly Lady ★★★★★

WANT TO BE THE FIRST TO KNOW ABOUT MY UPCOMING SALES, NEW RELEASES AND EXCLUSIVE GIVEAWAYS?

Sign up for my newsletter: https://www. subscribepage.com/byrdVIPList

Join my Facebook Group: https://www. facebook.com/groups/276340079439433/

Bonus Points: Follow me on BookBub and Goodreads!

ABOUT CHARLOTTE BYRD

Charlotte Byrd is the bestselling author of romantic suspense novels. She has sold over 700,000 books and has been translated into five languages.

She lives near Palm Springs, California with her husband, son, and a toy Australian Shepherd who hates water. Charlotte is addicted to books and Netflix and she loves hot weather and crystal blue water.

Write her here:

charlotte@charlotte-byrd.com

Check out her books here:

www.charlotte-byrd.com

Connect with her here:

www.facebook.com/charlottebyrdbooks

www.instagram.com/charlottebyrdbooks

www.twitter.com/byrdauthor

Want to hear about new releases, free books and get exclusive giveaways?

Sign up for my newsletter!

Sign up for my newsletter: https://www.
subscribepage.com/byrdVIPList

Join my Facebook Group: https://www.
facebook.com/groups/276340079439433/

Bonus Points: Follow me on BookBub and
Goodreads!

facebook.com/charlottebyrdbooks

twitter.com/byrdauthor

instagram.com/charlottebyrdbooks

bookbub.com/profile/charlotte-byrd

ALSO BY CHARLOTTE BYRD

All books are available at ALL major retailers! If you can't find it, please email me at charlotte@charlotte-byrd.com

The Perfect Stranger Series
The Perfect Stranger
The Perfect Cover
The Perfect Lie
The Perfect Life
The Perfect Getaway
The Perfect Couple

All the Lies Series
All the Lies

All the Secrets
All the Doubts
All the Truths
All the Promises
All the Hopes

Tell me Series

Tell Me to Stop
Tell Me to Go
Tell Me to Stay
Tell Me to Run
Tell Me to Fight
Tell Me to Lie

Wedlocked Trilogy

Dangerous Engagement
Lethal Wedding
Fatal Wedding

Tangled Series

Tangled up in Ice
Tangled up in Pain
Tangled up in Lace
Tangled up in Hate
Tangled up in Love

Black Series

Black Edge

Black Rules

Black Bounds

Black Contract

Black Limit

Not into you Duet

Not into you

Still not into you

Lavish Trilogy

Lavish Lies

Lavish Betrayal

Lavish Obsession

Standalone Novels

Dressing Mr. Dalton

Debt

Offer

Unknown

THE PERFECT STRANGER

**When he burst into my life, he set
everything on fire.**

He is a multi-millionaire, escaped inmate
serving life in prison for a double murder he
didn't commit.

He was once my only friend and my first
crush.

He doesn't ask for help and I don't offer.

**His hair falls into his face and a
strand brushes along his chiseled jaw.
His vulnerability is disarming.**

We both know that he shouldn't be here,
but when I stare into his piercing, intense
eyes, I can't look away.

I want to tell him to leave, but then he

leans over and runs his finger over my lower lip.

When our mouths touch, I know that I won't be able to stop.

What happens when one night isn't enough?

PROLOGUE - ISABELLE

I can feel my heart pounding as I press my face to the door. I can't leave. I don't know when I'll be able to get back to my normal life again.

These four walls are all I have. He puts me in my own bedroom and locks the door.

I let out a slight sigh of relief.

At least he didn't follow me inside.

At least he didn't throw me onto the bed and... You know how it goes.

It's every woman's worst nightmare.

No, that hasn't happened.

Yet.

All that he has done so far is put a

blindfold over my eyes and push me into my room.

My hands are drenched in sweat and my body is shaking. I'm all alone and yet I'm still afraid to take off the blindfold. I sit here, completely immobilized by my own fear.

My life has been full of fears even though nothing extraordinary or even a little bit exciting has ever happened to me. I like it that way.

I'm timid, and I'm quiet, and I'm the girl with her head in a book. Most of the time I get my coffee to go, but on occasion I venture inside and sit behind my laptop in a crowded room, just to be next to some people without feeling pressure to interact with them.

I have always been like this. I never wanted all that stuff that people on television want from life.

I never wanted a successful career up a corporate ladder.

I never wanted wealth and power, okay, maybe I want a little money.

I never even wanted to be a mother. Not yet anyway.

My life is super ordinary and I thought it would always be like that.

Until today.

I count my breaths. They are fast at first, a little bit out of control, but as the minutes tick by, they calm down. My breathing becomes more even and I stop shaking.

What just happened?

I try to replay the events of the day, but I get a mental block. My mind refuses to let me go any further back than the moment when I opened the door and saw him on my doorstep.

Perhaps, saw is the wrong word.

Who did I see exactly? I try to remember his face, but nothing comes to mind. He was wearing something over it.

A mask? No, not really.

It was something else.

A baseball hat hung low over his eyes and a bandanna covered his nose and mouth. His eyes were dark, piercing.

They should have looked dangerous but they didn't. Not at first, anyway, and that's why I hesitated.

I haven't had anyone come to my door in

a while. No food delivery guys or missionaries like the ones who came all the time when I was little. Do those even exist anymore?

Still, I should have known.

I should have looked through the peephole first. It's there for a reason, right?

I kick myself for hesitating. People don't just go around wearing bandannas over their faces for no reason.

It's eleven in the morning on an average, sunny Saturday.

What's the worst that could happen?

1

TYLER

I shouldn't be here. I don't belong here, but this is the only place I can go. This is the only way that I can get out of this mess and even then, I probably won't.

Still, I have to see *her*. I haven't seen her in years and if this all goes wrong, I will probably never see her again.

To protect her and to protect myself, I can't let her see my face.

She hesitates before opening the door when I knock.

I wonder if she will. If she doesn't then there goes my whole plan.

I wait, carefully looking around to make sure that none of her neighbors are around.

It's the worst possible time to be on a suburban cul-de-sac. The kids can come out at any moment to ride their bikes. A busy mom can load up her third row SUV for a soccer game.

I know this because this is where I grew up. Not exactly here, but not far from here with a stay-at-home mom who worked harder than most working moms.

She was the one who baked cookies. She was the one who invited everyone to sleepovers. She was the one who built the backyard swing set all by herself while my dad was flying all around the country, gone two weeks out of every month.

The garage next door opens and an Oldsmobile pulls out very slowly. My heart sinks. I turn my body away from them and lower the bandanna to my neck.

If they see me, there's a chance they won't remember my face, or at least it will be in shadows. If they catch me wearing this? I will be more memorable.

I don't know what they see or what they don't see, but they pull out of the driveway and slowly disappear around the corner.

Finally, she answers the door. Her hair is disheveled, long and stringy, pulled up into a loose bun on top of her head. Her skin is pale and white, dry in spots, like she hasn't seen the sun for a long time.

But it is her eyes that make my knees buckle. Almond shaped and piercing, just like I remember. Her lashes are thick and black and there is a little bit of a smudge of eyeliner at the corners. The irises are hazel, with a mysterious mixture of green and brown as well as specks of gold. She parts her blush pink lips for a moment and suddenly I remember why I am here.

I don't want to do this.

This is the last thing I want to do, but it's my only way out. I didn't kill anyone and I can't do thirty years for a crime I didn't commit.

No, I can't go back to prison.

2

ISABELLE

My heart starts to race.

Stop blaming yourself. This isn't your fault. It's his. You didn't do anything wrong. Why do you always do this to yourself?

I know that I am right, but the thoughts of everything that I could have, or perhaps should have, done keep flooding my mind.

This isn't supposed to happen. I am just a normal person trying to live my life. This doesn't happen in reality. This only happens to people on Netflix.

I don't know what is happening to me. I don't deserve this, but it's worse than that. I can't deal with it.

I can't even deal with normal life.

I don't like parties. I don't like going out. I'm an introvert and I like things that way. I'm happy with my life just the way it is. I have my schedule. I have my students. I teach little kids to talk.

I love seeing their progress and I love watching them get the words just right. This is what I studied to do in college and now I'm doing it. How many people can say that?

I work in a small office where there are three other speech therapists and I make a decent salary of close to $50,000 a year. Maybe it's not a lot of money for some people, but it's more than enough for me.

I don't have many expenses. I live well below my means and I save most of that income. I'm almost done with paying off my loans.

After that? Well, frankly I don't know what I'm going to do with all that money.

Maybe I can take a vacation, but then again, it would be easier to just *imagine* taking a vacation rather than actually taking one.

The thing is that I have certain fears.

I'm afraid of flying.

I'm afraid of driving long distances, especially at night.

I'm afraid of heights.

I'm afraid of wide-open spaces.

I'm afraid of closed-in rooms with too many people.

I'm afraid of speaking to groups of people.

On the outside, you wouldn't really be able to tell. I can hide most of these fears well enough so that you don't see the sweat on my lower back whenever I have to talk on the phone with a credit card company or God forbid a medical insurance biller.

The one time that my ex-boyfriend surprised me with a trip to Hawaii, I had a panic attack and couldn't get on the plane. Angry, he went by himself and met his future wife.

I'm not mad about that. Not anymore. We were never really right for each other, but he was there and it was convenient. After we broke up, I promised myself that I didn't need to be with someone for convenience.

I am perfectly fine by myself and dating

is not something that I am particularly interested in.

Maybe some people are like that. They just go through life alone.

I rub my hands on my legs and feel the week-old stubble poking through my unwashed leggings.

"How long have I been wearing them?" I ask myself.

Five days at least or has it been ten?

My heart is still rushing but focusing on things like this calms my mind a bit. At least that's what I have learned through my online talk therapy sessions.

Going in person is just too stressful.

I laugh to myself. India will never believe this if I tell her. I mean, of course she will, she has to, she's my therapist.

Of all the things that I have been afraid of and worried about, opening the front door to a stranger who pressed a knife to my neck was not one of them.

I take a deep breath and, with one swift motion, pull down on the blindfold. It gets stuck around the bridge of my nose and I grunt in pain. So much for swift action, I think.

I reach back and find the tight knot behind my head. It takes me a few minutes to get it untied.

When it finally falls into my lap, I open my eyes and look at my reflection in the full-length, stand-up mirror that's almost eighty inches tall and forty-three inches across. It cost $639 but was on sale from over a grand and it was a huge splurge. I decided to give it to myself as a present for my twenty-sixth birthday.

I look at the mirrored glass frame with a beaded border and an antique silver leaf finish that makes it look weathered and almost distressed.

Slowly, I let my gaze drift over to the center. The girl looking back who is sitting on the edge of the teal upholstered bench at the foot of her king-size bed looks small and insignificant. She has flat, mousy hair, sloped shoulders that will undoubtably form into a hump later in life, that is if she makes it that long.

I hear a ruckus on the other side of the

wall through the living room. Probably in the kitchen.

There's a stranger in my home. His movements are loud and all-consuming.

The walls of this house are well-insulated. It's a relatively new construction with wall-to-wall carpeting in most areas except for the bathrooms, the kitchen, and the dining room.

I wonder what he's doing making so much noise.

I wonder how long I have to stay here before he hurts me.

3

TYLER

WHEN I PUSH HER INSIDE…

As soon as she opens the front door, I'm not sure if I can go through with this anymore. She furrows her eyebrows making a little crinkle in between them. She looks confused and it makes me waiver.

I'm not the brutal killer that they described in court. I have never hurt an animal, let alone a person. Whenever a bug would show up in my house, I would cover it with a glass and slide a piece of paper underneath it to carefully take it outside. None of that stopped them from convicting me.

"I have to do this," I say to myself and push myself inside.

I cover her mouth with my hand. She tries to resist, but I press harder and she lets her body go limp. At first, this relaxes me, but then it makes me angry.

What if she was really getting hurt?

What if I was some stalker who was really going to hurt her?

She needs to fight. She needs to stand up for herself, but she doesn't.

Then she surprises me.

When I try to close the door, she reaches for it. She pushes me aside and into the wall.

She tries to run outside, but I grab her hand and pull her back inside.

"Don't move," I grind through my teeth, worried that she's going to recognize my voice.

"What do you want? You can take anything. Just… Leave me alone," she pleads.

"I don't want anything," I grunt in an absurdly low voice.

I want to scare her so that she listens and complies. I want to make sure that she doesn't pull away and doesn't try to get away.

What if she does?

I let my thoughts trail off.

No, I will not hurt her.

No matter what she does.

Not even if she calls the cops.

When I loosen my grip just a little bit she tries to run again. Perhaps, she's not as passive as I thought. There is some fight in her and I like that.

"Don't let anyone push you around, Isabelle," I say silently.

Unfortunately, I have to. I take the knife out of my pocket. Not exactly a knife but a sharpened end of a toothbrush. But when something like this is pressed to your neck, you can't tell the difference.

"Don't move," I grunt and push the shiv into her skin just deep enough, but not enough to break it.

Isabelle freezes on the spot. Her breathing intensifies, along with the beating of her heart.

I watch as blood pumping through the artery in her neck forces her skin up closer to

the sharpened end and then away from it
with each beat.

"Don't hurt me," she whispers.

"I won't, if you do what I say."

She nods.

The door to the entryway closet is open
and, in the corner, I spot something shiny.

I grab the satin scarf and say, "I'm going
to tie this around your eyes. Don't fight me."

She hesitates for a moment, but then
nods. I see her lips tremble as I tie the ends
at the back of her head.

Then I usher her to the bedroom in the
back. I pass one that looks like a guest room
but I take her into the one with the king-size
bed. She stumbles a little as she walks and
grabs onto the walls for support.

"Sit down," I say.

Again, she hesitates. I hold her hand.

It takes everything within me not to
intertwine my fingers with hers, but she
shudders away from me. She tries to pull
away but then thinks again and presses her
hand into my palm.

She's not doing this because she
wants to.

She's afraid.

She thinks I'm a monster.

Perhaps I am.

Perhaps that's what they have made me become.

"Here, sit on this bench and stay here until I say so."

I look at her one last time before exiting the room, wanting this moment to last but also not wanting her to know who I really am.

That's not true. Of course, I want her to know the truth. I know that she would remember me. At least, I hope so.

But I need to keep her safe. The less that she knows, the better.

I walk through the large carpeted living room with a mid-century modern couch and a gray fabric recliner to the side of it. There is southwestern artwork all over the walls, an odd choice for someone living in gloomy Pennsylvania, and books everywhere.

Shelves line all the walls giving the large space a much less cookie-cutter feel.

I smile to myself. Back in school, she always had a book on her just in case any conversation got too boring. I've always admired her for that. It's not every middle schooler who can just check out like that.

I wish it were the same way for me, but it wasn't. I was too busy trying to fit in. And once I was in? I was too busy trying to stay there, stay popular, stay relevant.

I walk around the kitchen, trying to figure out what to do next. My mind has been so focused on trying to escape from that hellhole that I have not given the best part of it much thought.

No one knows that I'm here and as long as that remains the case, I'm safe.

I glance down at the phone on the counter.

I doubt that she has a landline, who does anymore? This is her only way to contact the outside world.

"Good," I say to myself.

I hadn't planned to take her phone and the fact that I just found it here is pure luck.

I'll have to be more careful in the future. Luck only lasts so long.

I open all the cabinets and the drawers. I

look in the pantry. I search through the pans
in the cupboard below the stove.

What am I searching for?

Nothing in particular, just conducting a
general inventory.

I do the same thing as I walk through the
rest of the house. I have to know what is
here and I have to know what is not.

I check the garage last. A powder blue
Prius, a few years old, is parked in the
middle. The walls are lined with gardening
equipment, a toaster, a mini fridge, and
boxes of stuff that there isn't any room for in
the house.

How did you end up here, Isabelle? I ask
her silently. When we were little, you said
that you would never live in a house like this.
You had dreams of moving to New York, but
you were fine with Chicago and San
Francisco. So, what are you doing here?

4

ISABELLE

WHEN HE BRINGS ME FOOD…

Hours pass.

After the initial noise that came from the kitchen, silence falls over the house.

Is he still here? I sit on the edge of the bench for a while but when my bladder starts to hurt, I tiptoe to the master bathroom.

I debate with myself whether I should flush. On one hand, he knows that I'm here, so why not? On the other, I shouldn't make any noise, maybe he'll forget all about me. Eventually, I leave it alone and just close the lid.

Turning on the faucet, I wash my hands

in the sink. I look at my face in the mirror. I wasn't planning on going out today so I'm not wearing any makeup and I'm dressed in oversized sweats.

My closet is right over there and I wonder if I should change. Not to make myself look better, but dress in something a little bit more ready for battle. My heart sinks as I process that realization.

Is that what I'm going to have to do? Fight?

"Of course." I nod, saying the words out loud. "What did you think you were going to have to do?"

I pace around the room, trying to figure out my next move. I was so certain that he was going to come back and demand something from me.

The fact that he's not here is completely throwing me off.

What could he possibly want?

If he isn't here to attack me, why is he here at all?

My stomach starts to rumble and I realize that I haven't eaten anything all day.

Luckily, there's a glass on my nightstand.

I take it to the bathroom sink and fill it up. I drink all of it and once I'm done, I fill it up again. I drink two full glasses of water before I feel full.

I PACE around my room again. I wish that I hadn't left my phone out there and I wish that I had something else to watch besides my streaming channels. I haven't had cable in a long time and I never missed it, until now. I wonder if having access to the local news would give me more information about the intruder.

No, of course not.

He's no one famous.

He's just a guy who has barricaded himself in my house, but there's no way that any newspaper or television people would know unless I told them and there's no way that I can call the cops without my phone.

A landline would be quite useful right about now.

"Hey, are you in there?" the intruder asks with a slight knock on the door.

He's doing something with his voice

again, making it low and indistinguishable. He doesn't want me to know what he sounds like. But why?

Then it would be harder for me to identify him. Otherwise, he might have to hurt me.

My blood runs cold.

"You there?" he asks.

"Yes, I am." I nod, suddenly realizing that he can't see me.

"I'm leaving you some food by the door. Give me a minute before opening."

I give him ten, staring at the clock in the lower right-hand corner on my TV screen. Then I slowly make my way toward the door with my fists clenched and my whole body contorted in fear.

I turn the knob slowly and pull open the door even slower. I look through the crack and then down at the floor, spotting the plate. It's a bowl of soup with a spoon already in it.

I eat it at my desk, taking slow and deliberate bites and letting the butternut squash linger in my mouth. It tastes delicious. Is this from a can? Do I even have soup in my pantry?

"I would have brought you a napkin and some water and some other stuff to eat, but I couldn't find a tray to put it all on." The voice on the other side of the door startles me, along with his kindness.

"Okay," I say and then realize that would be rude.

"It's okay," I reassure him. "Really."

"Do you want anything else? You have some chips, cookies, and a few power bars."

"No, I'm fine," I insist.

"Okay," he says.

I hear him start to walk away so I clear my throat and gather my courage.

"Actually, I was wondering," I say with my voice going up at the end of the sentence as if I'm asking permission rather than demanding an answer.

"Yes?"

"Why…why are you here?"

He doesn't respond for a moment.

I wait.

Then I wait some more.

"Hello?" I ask, wondering if he had left.

"I can't tell you that," he says.

His voice is different all of a sudden. He had forgotten to lower it and…it sounds familiar.

"Okay, I understand," I say as nonchalantly as possible.

I don't want him to suspect a thing.

"Can I ask you something else?"

"Sure."

"How… long are… you planning… on being here?" My words come out jagged with long pauses.

"I'm not sure," he says, again in his lower register.

Did he realize that he had made a mistake?

I don't know the answer to these questions or any of the others rushing around in my mind. All I know is that I can't bring myself to ask anything else.

"Get some rest," he says and walks away.

5

TYLER

WHEN I MAKE A MISTAKE...

I made a mistake.

I don't realize that it was a mistake until I walked away from the door and stared at the plate on the floor.

I forgot to change my voice.

It was just a sentence, a short little sentence, but she could have recognized me.

Perhaps she did and she is just pretending that she didn't.

I'm not sure what to do. I have to stay here.

I'm hurt and I need at least a day, a night, to recover. I wasn't planning on staying that long, but this changes everything.

If my voice sounds familiar… If she actually recognized me… What then?

She's going to call the police and tell them what?

Of course, she will call them after, but now she can actually tell them who I am…if she knows.

I sit at one of her sleek gray kitchen table chairs with gold legs. If I could walk properly, without pain, I would be pacing right now. It was all I could do to hide this limp when I first got to her doorstep.

This all seemed like so much better of a plan back then when I was lying on my back on my cot in my tiny cell. I found out that Isabelle lived here a while ago and I hoped that she hadn't moved.

I considered looking her up again on social media during the brief access to the Internet I had every week, but I didn't want the trail to lead the authorities here. No, I had to take a chance and that's exactly what I did.

I use the ladle to pour myself a cup of soup that I made from scraps of vegetables I found in her refrigerator. There were a few cans in the pantry, but I was tired of processed food. I wanted to make something from scratch.

Alone in a kitchen with nothing but quietness and solitude around me, for a brief moment, I feel like a free man.

This is what life is like out here.

This is what my life would have been like if I hadn't been framed for a crime I didn't commit.

Anger starts to boil up within me, but I push it away.

No, I can't focus on that now. I need solutions and if not solutions, then I at least need some peace.

I take a spoonful of the thick gold and yellow butternut squash soup and let the liquid linger in my mouth for a few moments.

Seasoned with black pepper and paprika, it tastes nothing like the over-processed, over-salted shit they served us at the penitentiary.

I have had my doubts about whether or not trying to escape was a good idea. There is a high probability of getting caught and getting years of additional time tacked on.

Now, sitting in her kitchen, eating homemade soup that I made all by myself, it all somehow seems worth it.

After I place the bowl in the sink and wash it out, I sit back on the chair and look at my leg. When I first got here, I wrapped it up with a dish towel to stop the bleeding.

It worked, but I need a more permanent solution.

It's a gunshot wound after all. Two actually, but they are small. A bullet grazed my calf and another my thigh.

I roll up my pants leg to check out the damage.

I cut my pants open with a pair of kitchen scissors. When I pull the cloth away, a burning sensation starts to run up my leg. That's how it felt when it first happened. The wound is small, the round is long gone, but the damage remains.

The thing that's curious is that I didn't feel it hit at all and only noticed that I was bleeding when I was about two miles away.

Some people say that happens with an

adrenaline rush. I had so much other shit going on in my head that it dulled the pain, but after I got here and relaxed the pain came back with a roar.

I clean the wound by putting my leg on the edge of the kitchen sink. It burns like hell but I grind my teeth through it.

Luckily, the bleeding has stopped somewhat, but it would still be a good idea to get some hydrocortisone or triple antibiotic cream on it.

I check her guest bathroom, the pantry, and everywhere else where a first aid kit might be, but I don't see anything.

I go back to her bedroom and knock again. The TV is on low and she pauses it when she hears me.

"I hate to bother you, ma'am, but do you happen to have a first aid kit in there?" I'm careful to lower my voice again, but I wonder if it's too late.

"Um… I don't know, let me check," she says.

A few minutes later she says, "I have some bandages, hydrogen peroxide, and some Band-Aids. What do you need?"

"I'll take all of them. Just put them outside the door."

Perhaps, a wiser man than me would not have hinted at the fact that I was hurt.

It's not a good thing to admit a weakness, but I've never said that I was wise. Just a little cunning.

I smile to myself as I remember my escape from a maximum-security prison complex.

A prison escape is the stuff of dreams for any inmate as it was for me. We sit in our cells and we go through our days and we look for the prison's weaknesses.

We watch the guards.

We memorize their shift changes. We consider which ones will be the easiest to trick, to bribe, to buy.

A few of us think about ingenious ways of getting away without brutal force. You want to hurt them, of course, because of everything that they have done to you, but you also know that to escape, and I mean, really get away in that Shawshank Redemption sort of way, you have to escape without anyone realizing it. Otherwise, there will be news broadcasts and helicopters and police blockades on all of the interstates. This kind of plan was what I was after.

The supplies that Isabelle lays out for me are helpful. They'll help me stave off infection for now, but it would be good to have something sturdier to tie up my leg. I search the cabinets in the guest room and even check the garage for anything that would work, eventually finding a few strong tea towels in one of the closets in the garage. Relieved that I finally found something that will work, I come back into the house to a loud popping sound.

6

ISABELLE

WHEN I GO FOR IT…

The windows of my room are on the first floor. They open from the inside, but there's a screen on the outside to keep the bugs out.

I've been glancing over there ever since I put on the television, trying to figure out the best way to open one, sneak out, and get away.

I am looking out of the right one when I hear a knock on the door and he asks me for a first aid kit. My heart sinks down into the pit of my stomach. My hands turn to ice and I hold my breath.

He could've caught me. But doing what exactly?

If he had opened the door, he would've just seen me standing here.

When I collect the supplies from underneath my bathroom sink, I pray that whatever part of him hurts, it stays that way. Or gets worse.

When I hear him back in the kitchen, I turn to face the windows again. The blinds are closed. When I pull on the chain, the sun streams in.

The next step is to tug slightly on the rope to push them aside. There are two windows in my room, and one set of blinds is much louder than the other. There's something in the mechanism that gets stuck. The only problem is that I can't remember which one. I usually don't open them all the way, just twisting them enough to make it sunny inside. I tug slightly on the rope on the window next to the bed. They don't budge. I go over to the other window and try that one. This one opens quickly, with minimal sound.

"Shit," I say.

This is the window that is right across from the front and has a big bush in front of it. So, even if I were to get the screen off without making a sound, I would still have to climb over the five-foot bush without him noticing.

I look at the construction of the screen. It's built into the window, making it very hard to remove without the rest of the frame.

I try to think of another way. I crack my knuckles and tap my foot on the floor.

"For each problem there's a solution," I say to myself. "Just think."

That's when it hits me.

I could cut it open. I tiptoe back to the bathroom and find a pair of scissors that I use to trim my hair. Going to the salon and making small talk with strangers has become unbearably anxiety-inducing so I had given that up months ago.

I walk over to the window, glancing back at the door only once. All that I have to do is open it, cut the screen, climb out, launch myself on top of the bush, climb over it, and run.

Run as fast as I can.

I look down at my feet. The nail polish

on my toenails is peeling off, but more importantly, I'm not wearing any shoes.

No, this won't do. I won't be able to get far like this.

I walk back to my closet and put on a pair of socks and sneakers. Back at the window, holding the scissors in my right hand ready to cut, I take a deep breath.

This is it.

This can all go terribly wrong, but it's also my only way out.

I take another deep breath and press my fingers tightly against the bottom of the sill.

I hold my breath as I slide the window up. Without looking back at the door, I listen for footsteps and any other sounds. When I am almost certain that the coast is clear, I pull out the scissors and start to cut.

My motions are quick.

I start on one side of the screen and cut all the way to the top.

When I get there, I turn left, making a right angle slice through the mesh. I follow it all the way to the other side. Instead of tearing the rest, I continue to cut along the bottom. The screen flaps open in the breeze.

Now, there's no turning back. The screen is tampered. There is evidence of my attempted escape. I place the scissors in the back of my leggings, handle up, like a gunslinger in an old western.

Without any hesitation, I put my foot on the windowsill and jump up on top of the bush, as far out as possible.

The tops of the branches are spiky and sharp but not hard. The gardener was here a few days ago and he trimmed the top with a chainsaw.

It's not strong enough to support me and it starts to swallow me.

When I try to go through it instead, someone grabs my shoulders and pulls me back out.

7

ISABELLE

WHEN HE CATCHES ME...

I try to grab onto the bush and hold on but the intruder is too strong. He wraps his arms and body around mine. The branches swing back and slice across my face as I grasp onto them in desperation.

When we are inside, he pushes my head into the carpet and places his hand on the back of my neck.

"Why did you do that?" he hisses. "Why?"

He's not modulating his voice.

It sounds familiar. My whole body trembles as I wait for what is about to happen.

"Why did you do that?" he asks again.

I refuse to move.

I keep my eyes shut.

He doesn't want me to know who he is and I'm perfectly fine with that. I don't need to know. It's safer for me to *not* know.

"Do you know who I am?" he asks.

I shake my head no.

"Don't pretend," he says. "Do you know who I am?"

"No, I don't," I plead. "I swear, I don't know who you are."

Is he actually trying to keep me safe?

He put the blindfold over my eyes and locked me in my room because he didn't want me to know the truth. Was he going to let me go? Did I fuck that up?

Anger starts to boil in the pit of my stomach.

He was never going to let you go, Isabelle. Stop trying to take the blame for everything.

This has nothing to do with you. This is all about *him*.

He is the one who first came to your house.

54

He is the one who is responsible for all of the shit.

He is the one who is taking you hostage.

Nothing he did is your fault.

Trying to get away? Anyone would have done that. It would've been stupid *not* to at least try.

"I don't believe you," he says quietly. "You've heard my voice and you tried to escape."

I get a crick in my neck so I turn to face the other way. I insist I have no idea who he is.

"What do you want with me?" I finally ask when I get the sense that he doesn't believe me. "Why are you doing all of this? What is the fucking point?"

I feel his body loosen on top of mine.

I also feel the coldness of the blade in the back of my pants. He doesn't know that they are there. I still have a chance.

The first time that his grip loosens on my hands, I reach back, grab the scissors, and slice them across his stomach.

Startled, he tries to grab them, but I slice him again.

"Isabelle, stop!" he yells when I go at him again.

Instantly, I recognize him as the boy who was once the closest friend that I have ever had.

"TYLER? WHAT ARE YOU DOING HERE?"

He grabs onto his stomach. The blood has already soaked through his shirt and when he pulls his hand away for a moment, I see how much of it he has lost.

Suddenly, his face goes pale. He takes a step back and collapses onto the floor.

I don't know what to do.

Frantically, I cradle his head in my lap and call his name over and over again.

"Tyler, Tyler, Tyler! It's okay. It's going to be okay."

I say this over and over again but I have no idea if this is true. In fact, I worry that it's the exact opposite.

I don't know what to do. My heart is pounding out of my chest. I stare at his pale face that's in the process of turning some unnatural blue-green color and I freeze up.

I want to call an ambulance but then I'd have to explain what happened. I don't know why he's here or why he held me hostage but I know that he wouldn't have done this if he wasn't totally desperate.

I know this man.

I grew up with him.

He was my best friend in middle school; my only friend.

I carefully place his head on the carpet and run to the bathroom. Under the sink, I look for something, but what?

He is passed out.

I don't know how to make him come back.

At a loss as to what else I can do, I fill up a glass of water and bring it over to him. I dip my hand in it and carefully pat his face, but nothing happens.

I slap him. Then I slap him harder. My hand makes a loud smacking sound when it comes in contact with his skin. But he doesn't wake up.

"Tyler, please! Please wake up!" I yell over and over.

More blood oozes out of his wounds. I lift up his shirt and press my hand firmly to it. After taking off my hoodie, I tie it firmly around his body. When I push harder to stop the bleeding, suddenly Tyler opens his eyes and looks at me.

"Tyler! Tyler!" I yell.

"Hi," he whispers.

"I don't know what happened," he mumbles.

"You lost consciousnesses," I say. "You've lost too much blood."

He sits up a little bit, propping himself up with his elbows. "No, it's not that."

"Be careful," I say, adjusting the tourniquet against his stomach.

"You didn't get me that deep. I just have low blood pressure and sometimes it gets the best of me…" His voice trails off. "I must have passed out."

8

TYLER

WHEN SHE CATCHES ME...

I don't know what I'm doing here. I look at her eyes and wonder how it all went so wrong. It's not that I'm not happy to see her, of course I am.

It's more complicated than that. It's just that my whole life has become something of a blur, almost as if it belongs to someone else.

Hair falls into her face as she tends to my injuries, but she looks through it instead of pushing it away.

I'm tempted to reach out but it's not my place. It never was and probably never will be.

I knew Isabelle in another life, when I

was a kid who thought that the world was mine for the taking.

What I didn't know was that the world would chew me up, spit me out, and tell lies about me to anyone who would listen.

"No, not now," I say silently to myself. "This isn't about me. Don't make this moment about the past."

I look into her deep hazel eyes. She is completely focused on examining the cuts on my stomach. It was she who held the knife and I would've probably taken her much more seriously if I had known that she was not a complete novice with one.

After cleaning out the wounds and finding and applying some triple antibiotic to it, she carefully cuts a bandage just the right size and places it on top of the wound.

Pressing her hand against the wound, she looks at me as if she is waiting for some sort of reaction, but the pain is nothing in comparison to what I have felt.

I grew up in a violent home and after being thrown into a maximum-security prison, feeling physical pain is just something that I have grown used to.

After a while, your muscles remember. A lot of what comes with pain is mental. You get a cut on your finger and the unexpected flow of blood shocks you. It reminds you that you're alive and, if you are alive, then you can die.

But if you are used to getting those cuts, then there is no shock that comes with it.

It's just something that happens. It's like that with other types of violence as well.

You endure enough of it and your senses get dulled...for better or worse.

Without saying a word, Isabelle moves on to my leg. I'm lying back on her couch, leaning on one elbow for support.

"My leg is fine. I checked on it earlier."

"I think I can do a little better than this," she insists.

I'm tempted to fight her, but what's the point?

If she can clean it up again and make it a little less ad hoc then why not?

"Does this hurt?" she asks.

I shake my head no.

It's a lie, but what's a little white lie between friends?

She leans over me, looking closely at it for a moment.

The blood has dried, but it's still not a pretty sight. Now, it looks deeper than it did earlier. When I had cleaned it up, I did my best, but I was in a hurry without much energy or dedication.

Isabelle isn't in that headspace. She takes her time. She's patient.

She pours a little bit of the hydrogen peroxide onto a paper towel and then presses it into the wound. She is meticulous and makes sure that she gets every nook. A little too meticulous if you ask me.

"Does that hurt?" she asks in reaction to my scrunched up face. "No, I'm fine," I lie.

She gives me a weak smile. I know that she doesn't believe me.

"You know you don't have to pretend with me," she says. "We go way back."

She pauses a little bit as if she is thinking about what else to say to follow that.

She does know me, of course. We first met in sixth grade, at that unique time in our lives when we had not quite learned how to live with the lies that the world throws at us.

I have a theory about childhood. When you're a kid, you don't need to make yourself someone you're not. The only thing that matters is what you're interested in. But as you grow up, you start noticing that there are differences between people. Some have better homes, better families, or more love. That's when you start to invent yourself a persona. Everyone does this. Even the good ones.

Isabelle and I met at that special time in our lives when neither of us had started to pretend that we were something that we were not. You could call it innocence or you could call it honesty.

In any case, she knows who I am because she knew who I was.

"I'm not the same person that I used to be," I say, wincing again as she pours more hydrogen peroxide into my wound.

I don't know if she believes me.

"There's still something in here," she says, grabbing her phone off the counter and putting on the flashlight.

My heartbeat speeds up.

The phone is her way out.

The phone is the way that she can contact the authorities and tell them exactly where I am.

I stare at the blinding light and wait for her to dial the three little numbers, but she doesn't.

"Did you hear me?" she asks, moving her hand and throwing the light directly into my eyes.

I recoil and blink and see only spots.

"Yeah, that must be a bullet or parts of it."

"I have to get it out."

I shake my head no. "It has started healing already. I don't want to prolong it."

"It's not going to heal properly with this thing still in it."

"Sometimes they do," I insist.

"Most of the time they don't. It's going to get infected and this is your leg. You need your leg, right?"

I move my jaw from side to side trying to relax.

She's right. The problem is that I hadn't

spotted it before. If I had then I would have taken it out.

"Let me get some tweezers," she says. "I also have a needle in a sewing kit. I think I can wiggle it free without too much damage."

I give her a nod, but it doesn't seem to be necessary. She has already jumped off the couch and headed to the bathroom in her master bedroom.

I glance over at the couch. She has taken her phone with her.

My throat closes up.

I force myself to take a breath, no matter how small.

What the fuck do I do if she calls the cops?

She returns before I can decide one way or another.

"Okay, let me try the tweezers and then the needle."

She lays both of them on the armrest of the couch and carefully kneels over my leg.

Her phone is sticking out of the slim pocket of her yoga pants. On the back, it's yellow with little green flowers on it.

The camera is sticking out a little bit, but she hasn't made the call. Not yet anyway.

911 operators are obligated to keep you on the line just in case anything happens.

Then something occurs to me.

What if she is on the line? What if she's just pretending to have it off?

"I didn't call anyone," Isabelle says without lifting her head.

"I wasn't…"

"You're right," she says. "I see you watching the phone. I didn't call the police, but that doesn't mean that I won't."

"Is that a threat?" I ask.

"You can take it any way you want to. It's just something that's going to happen unless…"

"Unless what?" I ask.

She lifts up her hand and carefully pulls the tweezers away from my bleeding flesh.

She turns her eyes upward and meets mine. Narrowing their almond shape, she furrows her brows and glares at me.

"Unless you tell me the truth. I want to know why you're here. I want to know what you did. I want to know everything."

We don't talk the rest of the time that she picks out my wound. She needs solitude to focus and I need quietness to think about what to tell her.

Given everything that happened, it's surprising perhaps that I hadn't thought about this moment.

I mean, I knew that I was going to come here and hide out, but I never expected to bring her into this.

I thought that somehow it would all work out without her ever knowing the truth.

And now?

After picking out all of the fragments of the bullet, she pours on some more hydrogen peroxide and applies pressure while I clench my jaw.

"Now it's going to heal right," Isabelle says with utter confidence.

She applies the bandage, making it tight but not so tight that it's cutting off my circulation. She wraps the bandage a few times around my leg and adjusts it to make sure that it's secure.

"There," she says. "It should be good for

a bit but don't get it wet. I'll have to change it tomorrow."

Our eyes meet again and she shifts her weight from one knee to another.

"That is, if you are here tomorrow," she adds.

I give her a slight nod. I don't know the answer to that any more than she does.

"Okay," she says, standing up and sitting on the circular portion of the couch. "Now, it's your turn. Why are you here?"

9

TYLER

"Why are you here?" Isabelle asks, clearing her throat.

"I don't know how to answer that," I say after a moment. "What do you want me to say?"

"I want you to tell me the truth. I don't hear from you for years. Whenever I try to call you or email you, all of those messages go unanswered. Then suddenly, one Saturday afternoon, you show up at my door, put a knife to my throat, and you try to hold me hostage? Why?"

I look down at my hands. They've gotten bigger since I've been inside. In prison, I mean. These used to be the hands of someone who worked behind a desk. And now they seem to belong to a man capable of just about anything.

"I didn't want you to know who I was," I finally say. "I didn't want to hurt you. I didn't want to get you involved, so I thought that this would be the best way."

She tilts her head and stares at me as if I had just lost my mind.

"What the hell are you talking about?" she asks.

"I thought that I could break in, spend the night here, take care of my injury, and be on my way. I had no idea that I was going to get hurt; that wasn't really part of the plan as you can imagine. And then…then I just needed a place to heal. Since everyone is looking for me."

"Who? Who is looking for you?" She sits up on the couch and scrunches her shoulders inward, putting her hand on her knees.

I glare at her. Is she kidding? Does she really not know?

"The cops. They probably have all the highways blocked off."

"What are you talking about?"

I look at her and she looks at me and then suddenly it hits me. There is no light bulb going off above my head, but there might as well be.

For a brief moment, I consider not telling her the truth. If she doesn't know that I am an escaped convict, perhaps it's better if I keep it that way.

I quickly write that idea off. She'll find out the truth as soon as I leave and I may need her help in the meantime.

"I thought you knew," I say after a long pause.

"Knew what?"

"That I was convicted of a crime and I was serving time at a maximum-security prison."

Her mouth drops open.

A wave of concern washes over her face as she leans closer to me.

"What are you talking about?" she asks. "So, how are you...*here*?"

"I escaped," I say. "I ran away, I got hurt, and I came here. I didn't want you to see my face or hear my voice because I didn't want you to be accused of harboring a criminal. But your house was the closest place to the prison and no one would suspect that I was here since we haven't talked in years."

"But how… How did you even know that I was living here?" Isabelle asks after clearing her throat.

"You made a Facebook post a few years ago about buying this place. I looked up the address then to see where it was and remembered it. When I ran away, I decided to come here."

She swallows hard.

"I was surprised that you settled here since I remember how you used to feel about places like this," I continue. "I thought that for sure you would be away from Pennsylvania by now and definitely not living a few miles away from where we grew up."

"Hey," she snaps at me. "At least, I'm not in prison."

"Yeah, I guess that's fair." I laugh.

I guess she meant for that to hurt, but it didn't.

In prison you grow a thick skin and very few things that are said penetrate through.

"I'm sorry that I'm here," I say after a long pause. "I should not have come. I should not have gotten you involved. I hope that I can leave without you getting any more entangled with all of this than you already are."

"What do you mean?" she asks.

"I don't know, but maybe we can just forget that I was here. In case anyone asks."

It's an awkward moment to ask for a favor and perhaps I should have tried to do so earlier, but if the answer is no, then I want to know as soon as possible.

"You have to tell me more," Isabelle says, leaning back into the couch. "Why are you in prison?"

"They convicted me of something I didn't do."

"What?"

I don't want to tell her, but the answer is only a few Google clicks away. There's no point in lying or even obfuscating the truth.

"Double murder. They said that I killed my wife and her lover."

"And you say that you didn't?" she asks.

"The truth is that I didn't. I had nothing to do with their murders, but the police had no other leads and no other suspects. I was an easy target."

She gives me a slight nod. It's clear that she doesn't believe me.

"How did you escape?" she asks, crossing one leg over her knee.

"I can't tell you that."

"Why?"

"I can tell you later. I can tell you everything later, but first, you just have to promise me something."

She gives me a nod and waits.

"You can't tell anyone that you tried to escape. You have to tell them that I came here and you had no idea who I was. I put a knife to your throat and I tied you up and kept you in your room. If anyone ever finds out that we talked like this, that you helped me, that you fixed my wounds, things are not going to be good for you."

She shakes her head and looks down at her nails. They're short, but not so short like they have recently been bitten. She used to bite them as a kid, but now they look polished and shiny, covered in a thin layer of glossy polish.

"Why would I tell them that?" Isabelle asks, finally bringing her eyes to meet mine.

"If you don't then they're going to make you pay."

———

ISABELLE MAKES us some tea and closes the blinds, saying that she has some nosy neighbors who don't like to mind their own business.

She helps me over to the round kitchen table facing the backyard. The grass is bright green, illuminated in parts with quiet yellow light from the lamps positioned strategically all around the backyard.

The shrubs give the yard total privacy along with a few smaller trees and landscape shrubs near the bay window in the kitchen.

"You have a beautiful yard," I say, taking a sip of my tea.

"Thanks, but I don't know much about gardening."

"I wouldn't say that looking at this."

"It's called a gardener, actually a whole crew of them. They come once a week, stay for half an hour, and make everything look this pretty."

I start to smile but it quickly turns into a snort and a laugh.

"What's so funny?"

"You. I mean no, it's not that *you're* funny, it's just that… We are really grownups now, aren't we?" I ask.

"Is anyone really a grownup?" she asks.

I shrug.

"I mean, isn't that just something that you think all these adults in your life are when you're a kid?" She elaborates. "I used to think that everyone over the age of eighteen knew exactly what they were doing at all times. What I didn't realize was that you go through life without a clue. If you're certain and completely set in your ways, well, you're the most clueless of them all."

I laugh. It's the kind of laugh that starts in the pit of your stomach and only slowly rises up into your mouth. The only problem is that you shouldn't laugh like that when you have injuries to your abdominal muscles.

"You really shouldn't laugh if it's going to hurt so much," she says dryly when I wince. A few strands of hair fall softly around her face from a loose bun and she pushes it up to the top of her head by tightening the band.

"Thanks, I appreciate your support," I say, forcing a sarcastic smile.

"You know, we really haven't changed that much," I say after a moment.

"Is that a compliment?"

"No, just an observation. I thought that maybe you would. I'm sure that I have."

She shrugs and takes a sip of her tea. The mug is comically large, making her appear minuscule in comparison to it.

"I don't know if you have changed," she says after a pause. "I haven't heard about you in a long time."

"I thought that for sure you would've heard about me going to prison."

She stirs her spoon around the cup, making a loud clinking sound.

"I'm not very social," she says. "Not in real life or on social media."

"Yeah, I've noticed that," I say after a moment. "Why is that?"

I realize what kind of loaded question this is and before it even escapes my lips, it's already too late.

Perhaps, I can make an amendment.

"There's no way to really answer that without explaining everything about yourself, is there?" I ask.

"No, there isn't," she agrees.

10

ISABELLE

WHEN WE TALK...

He has ashy blue eyes that look almost cloudy in this light. I got him pretty good with the scissors so he scrunches up his face just a little every time he shifts his weight to absorb some of the pain.

I don't know what to think when he tells me that he had escaped from prison.

I know even less about what to say.

I knew him when he was a child and I feel a connection that inevitably comes from that, but I don't really know him.

Prison?

Maximum-security correctional facility?

This is a world that I have only seen

portrayed on television and even then, my viewing experience has been limited.

When I ask Tyler what he did, he insists that it was all a mistake. He insists on his innocence, but don't they all?

I ask him for more details but he says that he doesn't want to talk about it.

When I ask him to tell me how he escaped, again he shuts me down.

I have a feeling that the only reason he is here is because I remind him of who he used to be.

We have this history. It's undeniable and long-standing.

I remember him as well. I know that we were really good friends and for a long time he was the only person I ever really loved.

Things are different now.

He's a stranger to me.

He wants me to believe something about him that is completely… Unbelievable.

Still, I don't call the police.

While we sit together on the couch, he looks into my eyes. His face relaxes and there's an honesty there that is quite disarming.

I don't remember the last time a man looked at me like this, if ever. Tyler looks at me and it feels like he actually sees me.

"So, what do you do?" Tyler asks.

His tone of voice is different from the way that people usually ask this question.

It doesn't feel like an obligation, more like he is genuinely interested.

"I'm a speech therapist."

"What's that? Exactly?"

"I teach little kids how to talk. Some of them just have a slight speech delay. Others have serious neurological problems that prevent them from being able to say words. I work for a practice not far from here. There are a few other therapists there and that's pretty much all we do; teach little kids how to communicate."

"Wow, that's cool."

He looks genuinely taken aback.

"Are you surprised?"

"No, of course not," he says a little bit too quickly.

I wait for him to explain.

"Well, actually, maybe I am. I just

remember when we were kids and… All you wanted to do was write."

I shrug my shoulders.

"Do you not want to do that?"

"Yes, I still like to write, but that's not what I ended up doing. You asked me what I do for a living, remember?"

"Do you like your job?"

"Yes," I say with certainty. "The truth is that I do enjoy it quite a lot. I like my kids and I love seeing how they make progress. You have this little kid come to you at age two without a single word in their vocabulary and then with a lot of hard work, suddenly he starts saying ten, twenty words, even putting them together in sentences. That's the kind of progress that… Well, it's hard to explain just how much I love seeing the impact that I make on their lives."

"Do you have kids?" he asks.

I give him a blank stare.

"Do you see any kids around here?"

"No, but that doesn't mean that you don't have any. They could be away at their dad's."

He has a point, but that doesn't stop me from getting agitated.

Sensing that something is wrong, he apologizes.

"I'm sorry, I didn't realize this was a sore subject."

"It's nothing of the sort," I snap back. "I just don't have kids, why is that a big deal? Perhaps it's a normal thing to assume that a woman who works with children all day long would want children, but the truth is that as much as I love my clients, I don't really want a child. Not yet. I'm not even thirty and I don't have anyone that I would want to have a child with."

I don't want to tell him this, but it really irritates me how much women are expected to always desire children.

It's almost as if the whole purpose of our lives is to procreate. Men, on the other hand, get to pursue their interests, their passions. They end up having children as well, but there isn't this pressure on them to make families.

"Isabelle." He leans over, taking my hand in his.

His touch startles me and I jump back into the cushion of the couch.

"I'm sorry," he says quickly. "Shit."

"It's fine," I insist, speaking a little too fast. "You just scared me a little."

"All I wanted to say is that I'm sorry for being such an asshole."

I take a small breath and stare into his eyes. He tilts his head just a little bit and leans over. He is so close that I can feel his breath on my face.

"There's nothing wrong with having kids and there's nothing wrong with not having kids. It's a personal decision and I totally believe that. I… I don't even know how to say this, but I really didn't mean anything by that. I was just…genuinely curious."

I give him a slight nod and pull away, desperately trying to change the topic.

"So, what do you do?" I ask.

"Well, I actually work in the laundry room, making about… fifteen cents an hour."

"Cents?"

"There isn't much of a minimum wage lobby in the prison system. Whatever we get

84

paid we spend at the commissary where the prices are really inflated and our salaries are pretty low. That is, unless you have somebody on the outside helping you out."

"Did you?"

"I did, for a bit."

"What happened?"

"Umm…" He fidgets in his seat and now it's his turn to be uncomfortable.

"Okay, if you don't want to tell me *that* then tell me what you used to do… Before."

"That's easy," he says with a crooked smile out of the corner of his lips. "I ran a hedge fund."

"Really? Isn't that… Really expensive?"

"Well, I don't know if I would call it expensive. It required a substantial investment, of course. I also saved about $25,000 and my dad gave me a loan of fifty grand. I used that money to start investing in the stock market. The investments grew and after I paid back his money, everything became mine."

"Doesn't a hedge fund involve other people's money? Otherwise, you would be, what, a day trader?"

"Yeah, pretty much. I did so well that my old boss actually decided to invest some money with me and when he made a good return, he got his friends at the country club to invest as well. We eventually grew it to about fifty-million dollars, which isn't huge, but it's a nice boutique-size hedge fund."

"We?" I ask.

"Yes, I had a partner. I met him at my first job. We got to be close friends. He put some of his own money into the project. I was the one deciding on the trades and he took care of a lot of the client relations, like finding new investors, doing any accounting, that kind of thing."

I'm trying to hide my surprise, but my eyes are probably two big saucers.

"I had no idea that you were involved in anything that... Big," I finally say after a moment. "I mean, I knew that you were always going to do well in life, but this is seriously impressive."

"You thought I was going to be a starving artist?" Tyler asks, raising one eyebrow.

I shrug and give him a half smile. "You

were very good at painting and you enjoyed it."

"That's the funny thing," Tyler says, "I never stopped painting. It was the only thing that relaxed me during the workday. I don't know if you know but handling that kind of money comes with more than just a few pressures." His tone of voice is soaked in sarcasm and I roll my eyes in response.

"So, what, you painted? Was cocaine not relaxing enough for you?"

He laughs.

"Sorry, that's a stereotype, I know," I add. "Even though stockbrokers snorting cocaine is probably not a thing anymore."

"Oh, trust me," he says, nodding his head. "It's still very much a thing."

"Tell me more about your painting."

"I've always liked to do it and I just kept doing it after I started the hedge fund. When we made our first thousand dollars, I celebrated by painting a few canvases."

"No party? No dancing?" I ask, raising my eyebrows.

"Nope, just painting by myself in the guest room of my apartment with some wine, some Led Zeppelin, and a few canvases. When we made our first hundred grand, I did the same thing. And when I made my first million, only this time I set up a studio in my 5,000 square-foot apartment in Soho."

We talk a lot that evening, about everything and about nothing at the same time.

Occasionally, I forget how he got here. Most of the time it just feels like a visit from an old friend who got lost along the way.

I find out that Tyler went to the University of Pennsylvania for his undergrad and majored in Art and Economics. I tell him that I had hoped to go there as well, but I decided on Penn State. It didn't require me to take out as many student loans. I wonder if we would have met there, had I gone there. He seems to think that it would have been inevitable, but I'm not so sure.

"I don't really believe in coincidences or luck that much. I don't even really believe in destiny. The way I see it is that we are just a combination of molecules and atoms bouncing around the universe along with everyone else. Whatever happens or doesn't happen has nothing to do with us one way or another."

"No, you can't possibly believe that," Tyler says, shaking his head. "We are so much more than that and you know it. At least you are."

I smile, but then shake my head.

"Do you think that it is an accident that I'm here?" he asks, the expression on his face becoming very solemn.

I shrug and look away.

"It's not an accident. I'm here because I knew this would be a safe place for me to go. I don't know how I knew. I wasn't even sure if you were still going to be here, but I had to try. Something was bringing me to you."

"What if I wasn't here? If I had sold the house?" I ask.

"I don't know, but I didn't have many choices. Everyone else who lives around here is too closely connected to me and I'm sure that the cops have checked them out by now. You and I have not been in contact in years. I remembered your address. You just happened to mention it and I just happened to remember it. There's no digital trace leading me here after the escape. You were my best bet, my only good one, and with this bum leg, I don't think I could've gotten any further than your house anyway."

I give him a slight nod and twirl a loose strand of hair around my finger.

He's here because he doesn't have any options. Of course. How could I be so stupid? This familiar feeling that's passing between us that reminds me of all the best parts of being a kid, that's all wrong. At the very least, misguided.

The only reason that Tyler is here is that he needs me and he doesn't have anyone else.

11

ISABELLE

I decide to let Tyler stay the night despite my reservations. He's hurt, but he is still an old friend and he makes me promise that if the cops show up at night that I tell them that he had been holding me captive. This will add to his sentence, no doubt since kidnapping is a serious offense, but he doesn't seem to care.

Before we say good night, I show him to the guest room and tell him that the sheets are clean. He wants to take a shower so I fish out a towel from the linen closet. I never have visitors, so I only have one. Luckily, it's clean.

After showing him to his room, he

glances down at the phone in the pocket on my thigh. I wait for him to ask me to remove it, but he doesn't. If he takes it, I have my laptop, which is charging in the kitchen.

"I trust you," Tyler says after a pause. "Maybe I shouldn't. I'm probably being stupid, but if I don't have you on my side then I'm not going to get away with this anyway."

I walk away from him and close the master bedroom door behind me. On a whim, I decide to lock it. It makes me feel safe, but we both know that it's not necessary.

If Tyler had wanted to hurt me, he would've done it already. The fact that he's letting me hold onto my phone means he knows that I won't call the cops. It's reckless. He doesn't know me and if he wants to get away with this…

I get under the covers of my king-size bed and plug in my phone. While it charges, I search his name. I've been wanting to do this ever since he first told me that he had escaped from prison, but it felt like an invasion of privacy to do it right in front of him.

Now, alone in my room, I read every article I can find.

The details are not hard to come by. Tyler took off with two other men and their escape was discovered the morning of the thirty-first. Today.

According to at least two sources, there was gunfire.

Tyler McDermott was convicted of killing his wife and her lover, his business partner. After her death, authorities found out that his wife was pregnant with her boyfriend's child and suspected this being the reason for their murders.

I review the article over and over again, focusing on this paragraph. He didn't say anything about this when we talked.

In fact, he didn't really want to talk about it at all.

Could this be true?

Did Tyler really kill his wife, his wife's unborn child, and his business partner?

This has happened hundreds of thousands of times before.

I know, I watch a lot of true crime shows. It's always the husband.

Movies and television writers will make up elaborate storylines to have it be anyone but the husband, but in most cases, that's the real killer.

What about in Tyler's case?

His wife cheated on him with his business partner.

She got pregnant.

She left him.

He got angry and…

On television, it's such an easy jump to, of course, he did it, but this is real life.

Tyler?

My old friend Tyler?

Could he really do something like that?

I walk over to the sink and pour myself some water from the faucet. I drink the whole cup and refill it, placing it on the nightstand.

After crawling back in bed, I continue to read. I should have asked more questions, but now I'm going to find out as much as I can from the authorities.

Apparently, Tyler and his partner had a

falling out and he even accused him of stealing all of his clients and his business. One of the articles mentions that the partner stole the business away from Tyler and then took his wife. The writer actually uses that word, "took." It's so sexist and tone deaf that it makes me agitated, but I keep reading.

Another article says that Tyler found them together in bed and killed both of them.

Whatever evidence the prosecutor had, the jury believed him. Tyler was sentenced to life in prison. How he managed to get out and who his accomplices are I do not know.

I glance down at my phone. My fingers itch to make the call.

How can I *not* do it now?

Now that I know the horrible things that he was convicted of, how could I *not* call the cops? I open the keypad and stare at the numbers: 911.

"Just dial," I say to myself. "When she answers, just tell the operator what happened. You're not going to get in trouble."

That's the least of my worries. If the cops show up here knowing that he is holding me hostage, I doubt that they will let him leave in one piece.

So what? Maybe he deserves that.

A slight knock on the door startles me and I jump up, dropping my phone.

He tries the doorknob, but it's locked.

"You are reading about me," he says quietly. "Aren't you?"

"No," I lie.

"I'm going to go," he says.

This surprises me. I don't know where this is going.

"Why?"

"Why not?" he asks through the door. "You've read all of the horrible things that they have said about me in the media and now you're sitting there on your bed trying to decide whether or not you should call the police. I want to save you the trouble."

My blood runs cold. I don't know where to go from here, so I remain frozen in place.

"You should call the cops. It's the right thing to do. I don't want to put you out any more than I already have."

I don't know what to say, so I say nothing.

"Can you just do me a favor and give me an hour? I haven't slept much and you got me pretty good with that knife. I want to give myself a chance."

"Tell me the truth," I say after a long pause. "They said that you found them together and you stabbed them. Your wife was pregnant."

"I had no idea that they were seeing each other," he says after an even longer pause. "I saw them earlier that night. I knew that they were friendly, but I never suspected a thing. The first time I found out about her affair, the murder, and the baby was at the police station, but no one believed me. They all said that I was just a really good actor."

I go over to the door and open it slightly. I look deep into his eyes and try to figure out if this is true.

"Stay here tonight," I finally say. "I'm not going to call anyone. Then tomorrow morning… We can talk about it more."

I've picked up my phone and I'm holding it in my hand. He looks down at it. I see him wanting to take it away from me and then resisting the urge.

If he were really guilty, wouldn't he just take it from me to make sure that he's safe?

Then again, wouldn't he do the same thing if he were innocent?

I don't know the answer to these questions. What I do know is that if I were in his position, I wouldn't let me hold on to it.

12

TYLER

I wake up the following morning refreshed and actually surprised that I am here in one piece. The bed is the most comfortable thing I have ever slept on since they arrested me and I wish I could spend the rest of my days on it. If Isabelle were with me that would make the dream complete.

I don't want to read too much into my night, but I can't help it.

She had a phone.

She could've called the authorities.

She had all the time in the world.

Yet, she didn't.

Does that mean that she actually believes me?

No, it can't be that easy. In fact, I doubt that she does. Perhaps, the only reason she let me stay is because of our history. How long can I bank on that? I do not know.

I'm thankful for what I have right in this moment.

I come into the living room. It's still quiet outside, only a few birds chirping outside the window.

The guards make their morning rounds at 6:30, so I'm used to getting up this early. Apparently, Isabelle isn't.

I walk around the kitchen, wondering if this is my last day of freedom. No, I can't let myself think that. I have a lot more days to come, I just have to keep the faith.

Nevertheless, I decide to make breakfast. I appreciate what she has done for me and I want to show her my appreciation in return.

I open the pantry and the fridge and find some tofu and a whole bunch of vegetables along with spinach. I pour a generous amount of avocado oil into the pan and slice and dice the vegetables into little squares.

Once the oil starts to sizzle, I toss them in and wait for them to brown along with the tofu.

I've been dreaming of making a healthy breakfast like this one for a very long time.

I have spent two years and 127 days in a maximum-security prison with a lifetime to go. When I first got there, I used to spend days imagining my life on the outside.

What I would eat, the trips I would take, the women I'd be with.

But doing that day after day was bordering on masochism.

I couldn't do any of those things so I could make my dreams more realistic. I wanted to use the library a few days a week. I wanted to read in peace. I didn't want to exchange words or blows with any of the assholes trying to get a rise out of me.

Isabelle comes out just as the food starts to sizzle in the pan.

"You really didn't have to do this," she mumbles, heading straight to the teapot.

Dressed in a bathrobe, with a smudge of makeup and with her hair falling into her eyes, she has never looked more beautiful.

"I got hungry and I haven't cooked in a really long time."

"Do you like to cook?" she asks.

"Yes, it's one of my favorite things."

She sits down at the kitchen table and puts a fork full of veggies into her mouth.

"Wow, these are great. I'm not much of a cook."

"The secret is in the seasoning."

"Oh, so that's where I've been going wrong. I've just been relying on salt and pepper."

"Those are actually the basics, not sure if you need much more than that."

"Nothing I have ever made tastes this good with just salt and pepper." She laughs, taking a sip of her Irish Breakfast tea.

We sit together for a while without saying a word. Instead, I look out of the bay window and watch a little bird prance around on the bright green grass.

It's too early in the season for such greenery, but with the early morning sunlight and a few days of rain leading up to my escape, there is a new spurt of grass making its way above ground.

I expect her to ask me more questions. I wonder if she had stayed up half the night reading about my case and all of the horrible things that I had supposedly done.

If she did, she doesn't say a word about it. Instead, she sits across from me moving her head from one side to another.

"Are you okay?" I ask.

I don't want to stop gazing at the slight curve in her neck as she moves it from side to side.

"Yeah, I just get this tension pain in my neck sometimes. It started when I was in grad school."

"You were in grad school?" I ask, raising my eyebrows.

"Yeah, I got my master's in special education and Communication."

"Where?"

"Columbia."

"Columbia University in New York," she clarifies. "Why? Are you surprised?"

"Yes."

She takes that as an offense, recoiling a little bit into the seat.

"No, I didn't mean it like that, not at

all," I insist. "I was actually surprised because I lived in New York after college, when I first worked for JP Morgan while I was trying to figure out how to get the hedge fund started."

"There are so many times that we could have met and we haven't. It's funny how life is, isn't it?"

"It's almost as if we were destined to meet again."

"Maybe this should have been another one of those close calls. I wasn't supposed to be here this weekend. A woman at work is having a baby shower and she planned this whole trip to West Virginia just for her girlfriends."

"You didn't go?"

"No, I have a little bit of a problem about going outside and taking trips. Things like that. I was all set on going and then at the last moment, I changed my mind."

After we finish breakfast and second cups of tea, Isabelle turns to me and says, "Tell me about the murders."

13

TYLER

I don't know where to start, so I tell her exactly what happened as it happened.

"I came home," I say. "I walked into the house and it was late, around 10:30. Sarah and I had been having some problems so I hadn't been staying there much."

"Did you have another place?"

"Yes, I had my office. I had a couch there and I bought some linens and a comforter. It seemed like every time I came home, we got into another argument about the dishes, about me never being around. I got a bracelet for her with diamonds all around. It was for no other reason but to try to make things right, but she accused me of trying to bribe her. Maybe she was right."

I pause for a moment, waiting for her to ask me something, but she doesn't. When the silence becomes unbearable, I continue.

"I wasn't a perfect husband, but I never cheated and, of course, I never called her names or hit her. My dad did that and I promised myself a long time before I met Sarah that I would never do that to a woman, no matter what."

"So, what did you do?" Isabelle asks.

"I became distant and I buried myself in my work. I don't think we were ever really well-suited for each other. We fell in love hard but during the last year we really grew apart. She wanted a child and I didn't. It's not that I never wanted children. It's just that I had a feeling that things weren't going well between us and a child would just complicate things even more."

"So, what happened?"

"When I came home, the house felt... Odd. I poured myself a drink. I wasn't sure if she was asleep yet or not because it wasn't that late. I thought that maybe she was in the den on her iPad. I went upstairs and…"

My voice drops off.

I have told the story numerous times before, but somehow it has not become any easier. I feel myself detaching from the scene. The trauma of what I saw was so overwhelming that I can't relay the information without practically seeing it in third-person.

"Tell me what happened," Isabelle interrupts my flow of thoughts.

I focus my attention completely on her. Our eyes meet and I don't look away.

"I went upstairs and I found them. The light was on in the hallway but not in the bedroom, so it was hard to make out what I was seeing exactly. Slowly my eyes focused on her laying on her side. There was something dark and black on the white sheets. When I touched it, it was slimy. I later found out that it was blood. When I flipped on the light, I saw *him*. Greg. My best friend and business partner. I never once suspected that they had an ongoing relationship."

At this point, I start to feel nauseated. I lean over and put my head in my hands. I take a few deep breaths, trying to steady my heart rate.

"How could you *not* know?" she asks.

I shake my head without looking up at her. There's no way to answer that question.

"I just didn't. Maybe I was a fool, maybe I just didn't want to see it. I don't know what the fucking psychological explanation is but he caught me completely by surprise. For a moment, when I first saw them lying naked under those sheets, I got pissed. Angry. How could they be dead? How could they do this to me?"

There is so much more that I wish I could tell her.

For one, my anger was deeply seated. I was not angry just with them but also with myself and everything that Greg and I had built. I was angry at him and then I was angry at her and then I was angry with both of them.

Anger wasn't even the right word. It was more like rage.

But most of all, I was pissed off at the

fact that they were dead and that they weren't there to deal with the consequences of their actions.

"What about the baby?"

I exhale slowly.

"I had no idea that she was pregnant. The first time that I heard about it was at the police station where I spent thirty hours in a room with the cops, trying to explain to them what the fuck happened. They had different cops and detectives come in to talk to me and I kept telling the story over and over again. When it aligned too much with what I told the previous detective, they accused me of memorizing it. When there was even a small discrepancy, they said that I was lying. I couldn't win either way. Most of all, what made me the angriest at them was that they were wasting all of that time investigating *me*, questioning *me* about my whereabouts when they should have been spending that time searching for my wife's killer."

Isabelle nods her head in the same manner that one of the other female detectives did. Nodding as if she's listening, but really just waiting for her turn to speak.

"How did they tell you about the baby?" she asks.

I look up at her.

Our eyes meet.

She narrows hers and waits.

"This feels a lot like an investigation," I say. "Are you writing a report or something?"

"No, not at all, but if you want me to help, if you want more help than I have already provided, then I have to know the truth. I have to know everything that happened and I have to be okay with it."

I don't say anything in response.

"I can't help a man who killed his family, Tyler. No matter how much I liked you in middle school. I can't help a murderer get away with it."

I want to tell her that she doesn't really have a choice, but her cooperation would be much better and more effective if it were voluntary.

The thing is that it's not that I don't want to convince her of the truth. Of course, I want her to believe me, but what I really want is for her to just trust me.

Beyond everything else, despite everything that happened and what I have gone through, this whole thing is just exhausting.

I'm fucking tired.

I'm tired of talking about it.

I'm tired of justifying myself.

I'm trying hard to get people to believe me.

It's exhausting to go through life always on the back foot with a cloak of suspicion wrapped around you. Sometimes, you just want to be in one room with someone and have them believe you and accept you for no other reason other than they know that you could never have done something like this.

When I glance up at Isabelle and look into her deep hazel eyes, I wait to see the girl that I used to know look back at me.

But she is nowhere to be found.

14

TYLER

WHEN I HAVE TO MAKE A DECISION...

Isabelle doesn't have any more questions for me and I don't elaborate on the story much further. Instead, she takes out the first aid kit and looks over my injuries. She carefully changes the bandages, wipes away dried blood, puts on some more hydrogen peroxide along with triple antibiotic ointment, and covers up the wounds with a new dressing.

At first, I watch her meticulously check every cut but when she gets to my leg, I just sit back on the couch and close my eyes. This is a safe place, for now, and I will have time to be extra vigilant later.

With my eyes closed, my thoughts drift

away and meld with one another. The past, and the future, and the present all mold into one and become a mess that I can't quite make out. It's like an impressionist painting. It only makes sense a few steps away, as a whole, rather up close and in detail.

When I open my eyes just a little bit, peeking through my eyelashes, I suddenly become someone else entirely. I'm no longer a useless escaped convict lying on her couch.

Instead, I'm seven and I am sitting on a little chair that my mother had upholstered with fabric she got from a thrift store. It has little blue stars against a pale pink sky.

I'm injured, only this time it's my hand that's cut. I had thrown a baseball through the window in the backyard and I tried to retrieve it by reaching through the window.

My father is not home, but there is fear in my mother's eyes to how he will react. We both know how, but we don't dare say.

Mom focuses all of her attention on wrapping my cuts, repeating over and over again that she probably has to take me to the emergency room, but hopes that this will be enough to have them heal.

The broken window is impossible to hide. It leads right into the dining room and with the heat outside, there's nothing else to do but to cover it up with duct tape. My mother tries to use the least amount of duct tape necessary, but the broken glass is obvious.

As she works, she keeps shaking her head from side to side and my whole body starts to shiver. I'm old enough to know what's going to happen.

When my father comes back from work, he's irritated and agitated and in need of total quiet and a large martini. He doesn't want to be bothered and he doesn't even want a hug.

If everything goes well, then I spend the rest of the day in my room, playing as quietly as possible, which is nearly impossible given the hardwood floors and the thin walls.

Today is different. The window is broken and it's my fault. I've gotten a beating from the thick leather belt that's hanging in the entryway closet for a lot less, like accidentally dropping a jar of jam.

"Okay," Isabelle says, forcing me out of the haze of my memories. "You seem to be healing quite well."

I don't respond.

"Are you okay?" she asks.

I stare into space for a few moments and realize that being here with my future completely uncertain is still one hundred times less scary than that night when I waited for my dad to come home.

"How are your parents?" Isabelle asks as if she can read my mind.

"I don't know," I say, taken a little bit aback. "I haven't talked to them much since I was arrested."

She gives me a slight nod. "Do they still live in that one house? With the white columns?"

"The one all the kids called the palace?" I joke.

"I had no idea you knew that."

"The monstrosity cost one million dollars back then and not that many places around here had that kind of money. So, yeah, that nickname got around."

"They were all just jealous. Your dad

was a really big deal. Vice President of the company. Practically everybody around here worked for him in one way or another."

"My dad was a fraud," I correct her. "I didn't know it at the time. He made good money but he was a total piece of shit."

"Yeah," she says after a long pause. "Everyone knew that, too."

"I needed at least seventy-five grand to start my fund. I saved twenty-five, but I needed more. I didn't want to ask him for the money but eventually I did. Thought that he owed it to me given everything he'd put me through as a kid. I thought the hard part would be asking him for the money, but it turned out that the hard part was giving it back."

"What do you mean?" she asks.

"Well, he liked that I had to borrow money from him. That was the first time that I was ever indebted to him. When I gave it back three months later with the ten percent interest and a bit of bonus for a thank you... well, he didn't like that."

"He wasn't happy for you?"

"Did you get the sense that he was ever happy *for me* about anything?"

She shrugs.

Isabelle has met him a few times and as far as I know, nothing too traumatic happened, but he wasn't exactly friendly.

"Ever since that loan he never stopped talking about how I would never have the millions that I made without him. He credits all of my success to the loan and nothing else. If I hadn't made any money? He would probably hold it over my head forever, calling me a loser."

"I'm sorry about that," she mumbles.

"Doesn't matter anymore. I have not expected much from him in a long time. In fact, my conviction probably proved everything he thinks about me is right, that I am a loser, an asshole, a lowlife."

We don't say anything for a few moments and then she apologizes again for bringing up my parents.

I shrug. I wish I could say that things have changed since I was a kid, but in reality, they only got worse.

"Listen, I was thinking…" she says,

letting her voice drop off at the end. "Why don't you stay here today and tonight just until you get a little better and stronger?"

"No, I wouldn't want to put you out."

"You won't," she says. "The cops are everywhere. The roads are blocked off. They're looking for you and you need a good plan to get away."

15

ISABELLE

WHEN I REMEMBER...

I don't know why I ask Tyler to stay. It's just something that comes out of my mouth and I let it slide.

A part of me believes him. Yet another part doesn't, but for now, I believe him more than I don't, even though that's probably unwise.

I know that he's a convict who has been tried in a court of law. He has been found guilty. Am I totally ridiculous for taking his word over that of a jury of his peers?

I don't want to talk about his conviction anymore and neither does he. After breakfast, Tyler goes into the backyard and sees that one of my lights out there is not working. He asks if I have any additional light bulbs. I find a pack in a box in the garage and he changes it.

Afterward, he goes through the rest of the house and checks the other light bulbs. He finds two additional ones that have gone out in the foyer, gets a ladder out of the garage, and changes them as well.

At first, I try to stop Tyler from doing any of this. Not that I mind. I'm not much of a handyman and I'd let a few more light bulbs go out before changing them.

I appreciate his help, but it feels like something that he shouldn't be doing. He is supposed to be resting, but he says that this is a way for him to rest.

"I want to be of use and keep my hands occupied," Tyler insists. "Besides, this reminds me of being a free man. I haven't been able to do anything this mundane in over two years."

I throw my hands up, sit down on the couch, and curl up with my Kindle. I haven't had a man work in my house for a long time and the feeling is strangely comforting.

There is a kind of domesticity to it that

allows me to relax more than I think I have in a long time. He's caring for me and I appreciate that.

After finishing with the light bulbs, Tyler points out that I hadn't finished painting my master bedroom closet. It was a project I started a few months ago.

I looked up a bunch of stuff on Pinterest.

I bookmarked a lot of the pages.

I bought all the supplies.

I started painting, but then something came up and I just put it to the side.

I don't usually do that with anything but home projects. It just got too overwhelming for me to continue. It required an additional trip to Home Depot and after I bought more supplies, suddenly the momentum to continue disappeared.

I couldn't get into the right headspace again, so I just let it go. After a while, I stopped noticing it altogether until he brought it up.

"This won't take long," Tyler says with the confidence of someone who has done it before. "Seriously, it's not going to be a big thing."

"No, it's fine. I'll just get to it sometime… Later."

"Come on," he says, taking my hand in his. I try to walk away but he limps toward me. His movements are so pathetic that I can't help but cave.

"How are you going to do this with all of your injuries?"

"Slowly, but with great *pleasure*."

I bring out all of the supplies that I put away on their own side of the little cupboard in the garage. I spread out the tarp on the floor, covering the shoe cabinet and the built-in closet. Luckily, Tyler agrees with me that the cabinets are too heavy for him to move in his current state and I won't be much help. He doesn't like it, but he will have to paint around it.

When I leave him alone, I hear through the door that he had turned on the television in my room to a basketball game. I pour myself another cup of tea and plop onto the couch and bury myself in my book. When I look up again, it's almost an hour later. The game is still on and Tyler is still working.

I GO to the kitchen and make us some sandwiches. I don't know what he likes, but I like almond butter so that's what I make him. When I knock on the door, he turns toward me with a huge smile on his face.

"Wow, thank you so much." He grabs it and immediately bites in.

I look in my closet. It's almost halfway done.

"The paintbrush took me forever, but with a roller, it seems to be working at lightning speed."

"This looks great," I say.

"It *feels* great," Tyler corrects me.

"What do you mean?"

He shrugs. "Working on this made me forget about life for a while. My life."

He takes another bite of the sandwich and downs it with a few gulps of water.

"It's hard to explain, but doing all these things around the house, they make me feel normal. Like a regular person walking around free in the world. I haven't felt that way in a long time."

I give him a slight nod and after a few moments tell him that I'll be in the living room if he needs me.

The book holds my attention a little while longer, but when I finish it, I don't have the energy to start another one. Instead I flip on the TV and watch something to occupy myself.

Another hour later, Tyler comes out. There's a little bit of paint on his forearms and his shirt, but that's about it. He waves me over and I follow him to the back.

The closet is done. He even removed the tarp and the tape protecting the furniture.

"Wow, this looks amazing," I say, flipping on the overhead fan and opening the window.

When I sneeze from the fumes, he flicks off the light and pushes me out of the closet.

"Let's let this all dry first," Tyler says, rubbing his forehead with the back of his hand.

He doesn't want to admit it, but the

project has taken it out of him. He goes to the couch and sits down carefully, letting out a long sigh.

"I wish you hadn't done that," I say. "It wasn't an emergency."

"I know," he says after a long moment. "I wanted to. I missed doing stuff like that, working with my hands. Who knows when I'll get the chance to do it again."

"What are you talking about?" I ask.

"Isabelle, people don't really get away from maximum-security prisons. The ones that do manage to escape, they're always caught."

"Always?" I ask.

"There hasn't been one successful escape in fifty years," he says with a resigned shrug. A strand of hair falls into his eyes and he flicks it back. "Some people make it a few days out in the world, others a couple weeks, but that's it. They're always caught."

"Why?" I ask, barely audible.

"They don't have a car. They don't have shelter. They don't have any money. They have to commit more crimes to get any of those things."

"So, *why* did you do it?" I ask. "If you knew that you would get caught, why did you escape?"

"I didn't know that I would. I haven't yet, but chances aren't very good without a really solid plan, which I don't have." He tilts his head against the back of the couch and stares at the ceiling.

"Why did I do it?" he continues, lost in thought. "I saw an opportunity and I had to take it. I didn't kill them. I didn't do any of those things that they convicted me of. I couldn't stay there anymore. It was as simple as that."

16

ISABELLE

As the long afternoon becomes an early twilight, the tone of the conversation changes and becomes more lighthearted. Instead of talking about all the things that we don't have in common, we start to reminisce about the past.

Tyler is the first one to bring up Mr. Rosenblatt, the Spanish teacher who had a torrid love affair with Mrs. Ferrone, the chemistry teacher. There were rumors swirling around because a few kids saw them holding hands, but the story was officially confirmed when they were caught making out under the bleachers by the student body president, Deidra Leeks. Deidra never made up stories and rarely even participated in spreading rumors, so when the story came from her, everyone knew that it was true.

"The funny thing is that Mrs. Ferrone is now Mrs. Rosenblatt."

"Are you serious?" Tyler asks.

I start to laugh and nod my head enthusiastically.

"After divorcing their spouses, they married each other. They've been together for years."

"Are they still working there?"

"Nope." I shake my head no. "From what I've heard, they moved to Idaho and had five kids."

"Holy shit," Tyler says. "You think that you know people."

"Yep," I say. "You have no idea."

It takes him a moment to realize that I'm referring to him.

"Ha, ha," he says sarcastically, tilting his head. "I guess despite all of the rumors and all the juicy gossip that's been swirling around the people we knew growing up, me getting life in prison is as bad as it gets, huh?"

"You said you didn't want to talk about that anymore." I point out.

"Okay." Tyler surrenders, leaning back on the couch and adjusting the position of his injured leg. "Let me think of something else."

It's actually not very hard for me to talk to him and I imagine it's not hard for him to talk to me but tiptoeing around this subject is proving to be a challenge.

"So, tell me why you're here," Tyler says after a moment.

"What do you mean?" I ask.

"I'm just surprised that you ended up buying a house so close to where we grew up."

I look away, realizing that we have stumbled upon a topic that I don't want to discuss.

"You're alone, not married, no kids. Why live here?"

"You're assuming that I don't like it here."

"Hey, I have nothing against western

Pennsylvania. I actually didn't mind growing up here, but *you*, you always wanted to be somewhere else."

"I lived in a big city, New York, for two years." I point out. "It wasn't all that it was cracked up to be."

"Really?"

He wants me to be honest and, frankly, there's no point in lying. If I can't be honest with *him*, a man who I will never see again after tomorrow, then I can't be honest with anyone.

"My apartment was small and dark. The weather sucked, just like it does here, but Central Park was not enough nature for me to escape. Everything was really expensive and it seems like the only thing that anyone ever did was go to bars and clubs that all sold drinks that cost eighteen bucks a pop."

"You know, you're a girl, you don't really have to pay for them." Tyler smiles with the corner of his mouth.

"Yes, I do," I say quickly. "Otherwise, I'm stuck having a boring conversation with some asshole. No, thank you."

"So, that was it?" he asks. "You just didn't like the city life?"

I give him a nod, but it's a lie. I said that I couldn't bring myself to lie but here I am doing it.

The truth is that something happened in New York, something I can't talk about.

"After I got my masters, I just decided to move back. I would probably never leave the apartment if I stayed there because all of my money went to rent. Here, my salary is more than enough to cover the down payment and the mortgage for this huge house. Actually, it's probably a lot more house than I need, but that's okay, too. I like having a big house."

He smiles again and the way he does it, I'm not sure if he believes me.

"What about the weather?" he asks, refusing to let the subject drop.

I can't believe he remembers so much about what I said when I was twelve.

"Yeah, I fucking hate the weather here. I don't like the seasons. I don't like all the rain. I don't like the trees losing leaves. I hate how overcast it is, but mostly I hate the cold."

"Any plans to change that?"

I look down at my hands and pick at one of my cuticles.

"I don't know," I say, shaking my head. "Yes, I'd love to move to some little beach town in Florida or California or Hawaii, but it doesn't seem like it's a possibility for me."

"People do it all the time," he says.

"I know, but I'm used to being here. I'm used to my house and my job. I'm even used to the rain."

The truth is that my life is ruled by fears. It would be as easy as getting into a car and driving south or west to get away from this place. I could rent a new apartment, start a new life.

It's not like I have much of one here, but after what happened in New York, I can't. I've become this timid person that is afraid of her own shadow. I was always shy, but now I've become something of a recluse. I want to share this with Tyler more than anything and even now, I'm afraid.

"Hey, do you remember the first time we met?" Tyler asks.

Suddenly, I have a flashback.

My first class was music. It wasn't anything that I was ever really good at because every new music teacher that I had expected me to already know how to read sheets, which I had no idea how to do.

Of course, I didn't want to admit this, so I just stayed in my seat, never raised my hand, never told anyone anything, and tried to copy the answers from the girl next to me.

I don't remember much from my first day of school except that as soon as the teacher showed me to my seat and started the lecture, the guy in front of me turned around and made fun of my shoes.

It was March and my parents moved in the middle of the school year and I went to my first day of school in the middle of the week, and I had those shoes since August. The sole was coming off, exposing my socks, but that part was easier to hide than the big hole forming near my big toe.

I didn't say anything in response. I just ignored him, but when I discovered that he was also in my art class, it made me sick to my stomach. That was my first day there and that was what I would have to put up with for the rest of the school year.

The kid that made fun of me was Christian DeParmo. By his confidence and the way that he wore his hair (slicked back with a generous amount of gel), I could tell that he was one of the popular kids at school.

In our class, he sat behind me and I heard him whispering about my sneakers to his seat partner. Once she saw them, she started to giggle. Unlike the music teacher who didn't care, the art teacher simply didn't hear.

The only person who did was Tyler, my seat partner.

"You told the whispering kids to shut the fuck up," I tell Tyler. "I'll never forget it. I never had anyone stand up for me like that before."

"No," he says, shaking his head. "That was not the first time we met."

17

ISABELLE

WHEN WE REMINISCE...

I furrow my brow and say, "What are you talking about? Of course it was."

Now he starts to laugh and say, "We met earlier, by the lockers. You bumped into me, dropped your backpack, and all of these papers came spilling out. I tried to help you with them, but you refused. You didn't even want to look up at me."

"That was probably right after I had to check myself into the school and get the schedule, all by myself. My parents weren't exactly helpful with that kind of thing."

"Seriously, Christian is a total dick. I hear that he runs a used car dealership now, probably ripping off people just like he used to do back then."

"What do you mean?" I ask.

"He used to sell marijuana. He was one of the biggest dealers at the school, the only problem is that he was really cocky and actually started to cut corners. Like, he would say it's an ounce but it was less. He would mix the weed with something else to cut it and make it less potent. He would do anything for a buck. That probably explains his current line of work."

"Do you remember the papier-mâché project?" I ask.

He nods and says, "That was the first time that we got to spend any time together, just the two of us. It was my favorite project in the world."

I laugh. He was never this confident, cocky, and self-assured when he was a kid, but there were glimpses of it.

Tyler had asked me to work on the papier-mâché project for art class. He invited me over to his house because I told him that my apartment wouldn't work.

That was the first time that I'd ever seen

the grand mansion where he lived. From other kids in school, I heard the rumor that it cost two million, but I didn't believe that because no houses cost that much.

I hadn't been to that area yet. It was all stone estates and money. It was in the most expensive area of Pittsburgh, where there was a long history of mansions and money. The reason we ended up at the same school was that the Fox Chapel district included a number of poorer neighborhoods of which mine was the shittiest.

When he invited me to his house, I was supposed to bring my art supplies, but I lied and told him that I forgot them. The truth was that I didn't have any.

Art supplies were expensive and a luxury, and not something that I wanted to ask my parents for. Besides, there wasn't even any room in our apartment to do any art. It was only a one bedroom and I slept in the living room.

Tyler, on the other hand had, a whole wing of the house to himself. I'd never seen anything like that before. His bedroom came with a bathroom, a large walk-in closet, and a den. So, his TV, his couch, and his school desk were in a whole separate room away from his bedroom.

His room looked staged, like a home on a television show, but it wasn't a set. It was Tyler's house. This was where he ate, slept, and lived.

As soon as he came into his bedroom, he plopped down on a large beanbag chair, the kind that was always seen in an IKEA catalog.

"I had no idea that anyone actually owned these," I said, laughing.

"What do you mean?" he asked.

"Well, I've just seen them in back-to-school catalogs and college shopping catalogs at Bed Bath and Beyond, but I had no idea anyone ever bought one."

"Well, I did and I love it. It's really comfortable. Want to come sit in it?"

I hesitated, still standing awkwardly in the doorway.

"You know, you're going to have to come in here if we are to work on this thing together?"

Feeling even more awkward over the fact

that he pointed out my awkwardness, I inched my way in.

"Come sit on the beanbag."

As I approached him, I expected him to move, but he didn't. He barely scooted over to make room.

I didn't linger for long. It wasn't that I didn't want to sit next to him. I'd had a crush on him since my first day of school. It was just that I didn't want to make the wrong move.

We spent the rest of the afternoon working. Tyler had a big desk with lots of room for us and all of the supplies.

We listened to Nirvana, No Doubt, and Bush.

We laughed as we talked about our fellow classmates and we discussed movies in depth, analyzing every interesting scene and performance.

The hours flew by and his mom appeared a few times, bringing us cookies, lunch, and later pizza. She was thin, well-put together, and dressed in casual athleisure wear that cost more than most people's work clothes. She seemed nice and quiet, but a little bit detached.

That day, Tyler and I spent the whole afternoon together and my heart skipped a few beats every time our hands almost touched. I couldn't remember why but we decided to make a large octopus for our project. The tentacles proved quite difficult and became unwieldy.

We thought that we could do it in one day, but we were wrong. When I went back two days later, everything was different. His mom's easygoing demeanor was gone. She was nervously cleaning the kitchen and checking her makeup and clothes in the entryway mirror.

The house was spotless but the three boys went through it anyway to make sure they got every last bit of dirt.

"Is everything okay?" I asked. "Are you expecting someone?"

It felt a lot like they were expecting a king to grace them with his presence.

"No, yes," Tyler said absentmindedly. He went around his room and vacuumed it twice, checking the comforter to make sure that it didn't have a single piece of lint on it anywhere.

And I thought my parents were tough. I'd never seen anything like that before.

"I thought that we were going to work on the project," I said. "Do you want me to come back later?"

"No." He shook his head. "We have to get it done. It's due tomorrow."

If he was worried about dirt and making a mess, papier-mâché was not the thing to do. But he was right, we were running out of time.

"My dad was supposed to be home later, but now he's coming at five," Tyler said, anxiously glancing at the clock. "Let's try to get it done by 4:30 so that I can clean everything up."

I wanted to ask him more. I wanted to demand an explanation, but we weren't that close yet. We were friends, acquaintances, but this seemed like way too personal of a subject to approach.

The octopus' head turned out to be triangular and circular, at the same time, and the tentacles were a little bit too fat, but overall the project came out well. We finished by 4:15 exactly and as soon as we were done, Tyler started to clean.

I didn't know it at the time, but Tyler, his mom, and his two brothers were living two separate lives. There were two weeks of the month when everything was good and everyone was happy. Then there were two weeks when his dad was home from his business trips and everyone walked on a razor's edge.

That day, I felt his nervousness and anxiety. When I left that pristine, multi-million dollar home with those grand columns, manicured hedges, and beautiful gardens, I realized that perhaps the people that had everything in the world didn't have much except for money.

I used to think that my life would be better if I had just a little bit more security, but now I know that security is not something you can simply buy. It's something that your family has to create.

All of these years later, Tyler and I talk a little bit about that papier-mâché project, but we focus mainly on that first evening together. I don't bring up his dad and he doesn't either.

"You know, I had quite a crush on you back then," I say.

"You did?" he asks. "I did, too."

"Really?" I gasp.

"You didn't know?" He raises his eyebrows.

I shake my head no.

"I was certain that there was no way you would ever be interested in someone like me."

"Someone like *you*? What are you talking about? You were one of the most popular kids at our middle school. All the girls were into you and you knew it."

"Okay, I'll give you that," Tyler says with a wink. "All the girls were into me but I didn't think you were. And you were the only one I wanted."

I roll my eyes, not believing that for a moment.

18

ISABELLE

He stays here for a few moments while I twirl the silver ring with an infinity sign around my ring finger. It's smooth and cool to the touch and I like the way it feels under my fingertips.

"Where did you get that?" Tyler asks. "It's beautiful."

"At a thrift store in Oakland. It's run by this gorgeous woman with dreadlocks who drapes different colored scarfs around her neck. In addition to selling curtains made of beads and brightly-colored maxi dresses, she also does palm readings and tells you your future."

"I like that," he says. "What did she say?"

"You don't need to humor me," I say with a half-smile. "I know that you're not into that kind of thing."

"You don't know anything about me."

I lift one of my eyebrows and wait for him to explain.

"Hey," he says, raising his hands up in the sign of giving up. "It's true. You don't know anything. You didn't even know that I was sentenced to life in prison."

"Okay," I say, giving in. "Let me rephrase that. I *doubt* that you are into that sort of thing."

"Well, I can't say that I am, but I find a lot of things quite interesting. Stop avoiding the question. What did she say when you got your palm read?"

I shake my head.

"What?"

"I didn't do it. I was too nervous. I wanted to, but I felt uncomfortable. Awkward. I wasn't sure how it was going to go, what she would say, or how much I was supposed to tip, so I didn't do it. Instead, I just looked through the jewelry cabinet and when I saw this ring, I bought it."

"Can I see it?" he asks.

I pull it off my ring finger and hand it to him. He lifts it up to his face, examining it closely.

"It's beautiful. Stunning."

"Thank you," I say. "It's one of my favorites."

I'm about to open my mouth and say something when a loud knock on the door startles me.

My eyes get wide. I don't know what to do. Tyler stares at me, also frozen in place.

The loud knock is followed by another and another.

"Isabelle? Open the door, Isabelle!"

"Who is that?" Tyler whispers.

"It sounds like my neighbor, Pam." I try to remember her last name, but nothing comes to mind.

"She has a golden retriever and a bulldog," I add.

The information is utterly useless, but I have had a number of conversations, all small talk, while she had been walking her dogs. If it weren't for the dogs, I doubt that I would have even said anything more than a brief hello.

"Isabelle! I know you are home! Your car's home. I need to talk to you."

"Shit," I whisper.

I had completely forgotten that I have four small windows in the garage door and I guess she must have looked through it to see if I was home.

This is very uncharacteristic of her. She isn't the nosy type. I have no choice but to answer. I start to walk to the door, but Tyler stops me.

"No, you can't," he says, shaking his head.

"I have to."

Pam continues to knock and they become more and more urgent than the last. I get up and start to walk toward the door. Tyler follows me.

"I won't say anything," I whisper to him and then point to the two slats of windows on either side of the front door.

If he makes another move forward, she'll see him.

"Hey, what's up?" I ask, stretching my arm above my head and yawning loudly. "I was asleep."

"I'm so sorry to wake you," she says.

Pam is a fit woman in her fifties with an expensive haircut and manicured acrylic nails. I can't remember what she said she does for a living, but she works from home in her office, wearing leggings and different sweatshirts as a uniform.

"I haven't seen you for a while and I just wanted to see if you're okay." Her breaths are a little bit quickened.

"I'm fine. Why? What's going on?"

"Well, you have heard of the guys who escaped from the prison, right?"

I give her a nod and say, "Yeah, they've been showing it on the news."

"Well, apparently, one of them is from this area. Grew up in Fox Chapel. So, they're blocking off all the roads and checking all the cars. When I went to Target this morning, I had to show my ID to the cops. That was the first time I've had to do that, *ever*."

I feel the blood drain away from my face

so I yawn to hide whatever discoloration may have happened.

"So, they are blocking the streets?"

She nods.

"I haven't been out since I got off work on Friday," I say. "I think I'm coming down with something."

"Well, if you venture outside, don't forget your driver's license. They're stopping each and every car. They have a cop right outside the subdivision and then one near the plaza. There's a ton of traffic and cops are everywhere."

"Oh my God," I say quietly.

"I know," she says, shaking her head. "Well, I'll go but why don't we exchange numbers, just in case?"

I hesitate and then decide that is probably the best thing. "Yes, sure, of course."

We have exchanged numbers before, when I first moved in, but she has since changed phones and not all of her contacts were transferred over.

She texts the number that I give her to

make sure she put it in right and then asks if I want to come over for dinner.

I shake my head no and feign a cough into the crook of my elbow.

"Maybe some other time?" she suggests, backing away, and wishing me good luck.

19

TYLER

WHILE I WAIT...

I kneel down behind the couch while Isabelle answers the door. I know that I'm taking my chances but I have believed her so far and hope that this continues to be a good decision.

Their voices are loud enough for me to hear and I slowly start to relax. Isabelle is not saying anything and she's not sending any signals.

I listen to the neighbor talk about how scary it is that there is someone on the loose and Isabelle agrees with her.

My heart beats faster and faster. My life is in her hands, but when has *that* not been the case over the last twenty-four hours?

These kinds of things are going to keep happening.

This is just a neighbor who knows nothing about me showing up and throwing my life into disarray. But what's going to happen when there's a real danger?

What's going to happen when a police officer pulls me over?

What's going to happen when someone recognizes me from my mug shot that's all over the fucking news?

I don't think this is going to end well for me. But what choice did I have? I couldn't keep sitting in that cell when I saw an opportunity to run away.

I had to take a chance.

I'm innocent. I didn't do any of those things they said. I didn't kill anyone and I would never kill my wife.

So, what happens now?

How do I get away from here? I hear bits of their conversation. The roads are blocked and cops are behind barricades checking IDs… What do I do?

What's my way out?

Maybe this is it.

Whatever happens, it's not going to be good and Isabelle shouldn't get more involved in this than she already is.

As I listen to her talk to her neighbor from behind the couch, I marvel at how little her voice has changed.

We met in seventh grade and we decided to go to our eighth grade dance together. I remember asking her and she said yes, but it wasn't an official invitation.

It was all very casual, even though I wanted to go to the dance with her more than anything. Secretly, I knew that she wanted to go to the dance with me, too.

That's the funny thing about being that age. You both want the same thing. You both care about each other as much as two people possibly can and yet you're too afraid to let your feelings be known.

Why? Why was it so hard to expose your heart to another person? Fear of rejection.

Isabelle said that she didn't want it to be a date so I couldn't come to her house and pick her up as if it were one. I didn't really care because it felt like a date and if we could spend some time together before hand then I was only happier.

Well, it just so happened that my dad came home from work that day at five, his usual time. I thought I had done everything, but I was so preoccupied with my non-date date that I forgot something.

Isabelle and I were hanging out in the basement when he called me up to the kitchen. By the tone of his voice, I already knew that something was up, I just didn't know what.

I tried to apologize immediately when I saw that I didn't unload the dishwasher, but it was already too late. He wouldn't hear anything of it. Instead, he started yelling at me, calling me names. I was angry and embarrassed.

How dare he ruin my night after ruining every other important day from my childhood? That was the first time that I ever fought back. I was always so fearful, but that time I was more embarrassed and mortified than I was afraid of the physical violence that he would undoubtably unleash.

"Fuck you!" I yelled at the top of my lungs. "You don't get to tell me what to do, you asshole!"

The words had just escaped my lips and the look on my father's face said it all. He was shocked by my reaction. I had two older brothers and they had not stood up to him that much up to this point.

Long story short, as soon as I called him an asshole, he jumped toward me, grabbed me by my hair, and pushed me down the stairs. My body bounced all the way down, leaving bruises all over my arms, legs, and ribs.

I didn't know this at the time, but people have died from things like that. I have met guys in prison who have pushed their girlfriends and wives down the stairs with mortal results. I wasn't so lucky, or perhaps I was.

Luckily, my father had already had a few beers and he didn't follow me down to the basement. I didn't bother waiting. Isabelle and I left through the back entrance and we spent hours in the park not far away from my home holding each other and sobbing.

Mostly it was she who had held me and consoled me and told me that everything was going to be okay.

One of my biggest regrets in life is that when I had my head buried in her arms, I didn't lift it up and kiss her. She kissed my forehead and cheeks and held me softly, but if there is one thing that I would change about how my life turned out (besides coming home alone and finding my wife and her lover stabbed in our bed), it would be *not* kissing Isabelle that night.

I should have done it.

It was the right moment.

The moonlight was shining brightly above us. She was holding me. She was trying to make me feel better. Everything about that moment was as romantic as it could possibly be except for one thing; I was too much of a wimp to just go for it.

I don't know why my thoughts drifted to that night, but I suspect that it has something to do with how she's doing the exact same thing now.

This time it's not physical but she's

standing there and protecting me, nevertheless.

How far is she willing to go to save me?

But more importantly, how far am I willing to let her go to help me?

20

TYLER

WHILE I LISTEN…

After Isabelle closes the door, she walks over to the couch and looks at me.

"Thank you," I say quietly, standing up.

She shakes her head. There's an inkling of anger in her eyes that quickly morphs into rage.

When I approach to give her a hug, she shakes her head and walks away.

I follow her into the master bedroom at the end of the hallway, where we can be alone again. She turns toward me and her eyes waiver from disappointment to hate.

"I'm not going to keep doing that for you," she whispers through pursed lips. "I can't do this. You just showed up here and now I have to lie. What if that had been a cop?"

"I know," I say, taking a step toward her. "I'm really sorry. I didn't even want you to know who I was. I wanted to protect you."

"No," she says, pointing her finger in my face. "You didn't want to protect me. If you had wanted to protect me, then we wouldn't be here in the first place. You wouldn't be here at all."

I want to take a step away from her, but something keeps me here as if I am bolted to the floor.

She's right, of course she's right.

"Why did you come here? What do you want from me?" Isabelle takes a step away, but instead of turning and running away, she just raises her hands and buries her face in them.

"I know it's not fair," I say, reaching over and brushing her messy hair out of her face. "I shouldn't have come. I shouldn't have gotten you involved, but I didn't have anyone else. I'm on the run and this is the only place where I knew no one would find me."

"Yeah, until they do," she says, her eyes look up at me.

Suddenly, it doesn't feel like we're fighting about this at all. Suddenly, all of this tension that exists between us feels like it belongs here for another reason.

I look into her eyes and see a small reflection of myself. Only I'm not the weak, injured man who stands here before her.

I'm strong, powerful, and confident. I'm the man that I always thought she saw me for.

In return, I don't see the fearful little girl who seems to be afraid of her own shadow. Instead, the woman in front of me is equally strong, powerful, and capable of taking care of herself under the worst of circumstances.

Isabelle takes a deep breath, exhaling slowly. My eyes wander down to her lips and watch as they part. Our eyes meet again, but only for a moment. Then suddenly, my mouth looks for hers. Our lips touch and I push her up against a wall.

My hands are forceful, but my lips are

soft. After I kiss her, I pull away ever so slightly. I won't let anything happen that she doesn't want.

I wait for a moment.

I open my eyes and look at her.

She looks up at me and when I don't make another move, she leans over and presses her lips onto mine.

It doesn't take long for our tongues to find one another's. Suddenly, our worlds collide like pieces of a puzzle put together for the first time. There's a spot for every piece as if everything that has happened has been for a reason.

I kiss her neck softly, trailing my tongue up and down toward her shoulder and then back up again. I can feel her shiver, her body moving slightly up and down with each breath. By the time I kiss behind her ear, she starts to relax a little bit.

Her blouse comes off quickly, but she hesitates a little bit when I reach for her bra.

"Please don't do anything you don't want to do," I say.

. . .

SHE LOOKS up at me with her big hazel eyes, hesitating for only a moment and then reaching over and kissing my lower lip. I kiss her back as she tugs at my shirt.

When I pull it over my head, she looks at me in a completely different way. The careful gaze of a concerned medic disappears and is quickly replaced by a woman who is full of lust. She wants me as much as I want he.

The last person who looked at me like this was my wife but we hadn't been intimate for a long time. Even when we were, there was a perfunctory aspect to it, something that had a lot less to do with lust than love. Then, after a while, there wasn't even any love left.

"Are you okay?" Isabelle asks with a concerned look on her face.

Clearly, I have allowed myself to drift into another world for a little too long.

"Yes, I am." I reach over and try to kiss her again, but she pulls away.

"I don't want you to do anything you don't want to do," she says. "I know that

you've been through a lot. This is all very…
Emotional."

"No," I say, shaking my head. "It has
nothing to do with that. I want you. More
than I ever really wanted anything, except
my freedom."

She licks her lips and unclasps her bra.
Her breasts fall forward. They are not small
and they're not particularly big. They are the
perfect fit for my hands and I reach over and
cup each one.

They feel soft and tender and her nipples
perk up between my fingers. I reach down
and take one in my mouth. I feel her back
arch away from me, her hair falling away
from her shoulders.

After lying down on the bed, I tug
slightly at her leggings and pull both them
and her panties down at the same time.
She's surprised by my move, but I'm not.
I've been wanting to do this ever since I first
saw her. Hell, it has been longer than that. I
wanted to do this probably since we were
teenagers.

I stand up for a moment, looking at her
beautiful body that she is for some reason

trying to cover up with her hands. I drop my pants. She sits up and waits for me to come closer. I climb on top of her, cradling her head, and kissing her forehead around the angles of her cheeks, her chin, down her neck, and then back up to her lips.

I lose myself in her and she loses herself in me. This is probably not love, but lust, but it's the first positive emotion that I have felt in more than two years and the feeling is overwhelming.

"Do you have something?" she asks.

Shit.

I shake my head.

"Of course," she says, slightly embarrassed. "Why would you? It's not like they have condoms in prison."

"I understand if you don't—" I start to say but she puts her index finger over my lips.

Wrapping herself up in the blanket at the bottom of the bed, she runs over to the bathroom and opens the bottom drawer in between two Jack and Jill sinks.

Isabelle comes back with a little silver square and hands it to me. When she kisses me again, I pull off the cover and pull her on top of me. I unwrap the condom, slip it on, and then push her body on top of me.

My back arches and I lean up to kiss her as she starts to move her hips up and down. I get deeper and deeper. I feel like she is consuming me more and more and my head starts to spin.

When it feels like she's getting tired, I flip her over and get on top. She grabs my buttocks, one in each hand, squeezing tightly, and guides me deeper inside.

"This feels so good," she mumbles as I nibble on her earlobe.

Every time I get closer to it, I slow down, trying to last longer. I want her to come first. A few moments later, just as she arches her back and grabs fistfuls of the bedsheets in each hand, I watch her clench herself around me and yell my name.

A few thrusts later, an explosion charges through my body and I moan her name as I fall on top of her.

21

ISABELLE

WHEN WE KISS…

A small part of me thought that maybe there was something between us, but the kiss still took me by surprise. It was like a tsunami wave. It is only afterward that I notice that there had been all of these signs. Afterward, as I lie there in his arms, I feel dumbfounded. It's almost as if this whole thing happened to someone else.

"Thank you," Tyler says quietly.

I look up at him and see him staring at the ceiling. His eyes slowly meet mine.

"No, thank you," I say.

A small smile forms at the corner of his lips and I smile along with him.

"That was… Unexpected."

"More than unexpected," I add.

I don't know what to think about what just happened. I have never been so overwhelmed by my emotions before. Everything else in my life has been carefully plotted and planned. Even something as easy as going to the grocery store has become a checklist of things that I do, and the days and the specific time that I do it.

I have gotten so used to going through life by following a strict set of rules all in an effort to diminish my anxiety that I had completely forgotten what it's like to simply do as you please.

After talking to Pam, I was so angry with him. I was angry at him for a variety of reasons but mostly because he was still this wonderful person that I remember who was my best friend when I was a kid, my only friend, and now he had to hide out in my living room while the state police have blocked off roads in search of him.

I don't know if that emotion was wrong or if there is even a wrong emotion. Isn't it something that just happens?

But then…what happened then? Somehow that anger morphed into something else. When I looked at him and I saw him looking at me, I wanted him to kiss me more than I ever wanted anything.

I didn't think that he actually would and when he did, I just let myself go. I kissed him back. Our lips found each other's and that was the beginning of everything.

Lying here now, next to him, my old familiar worries start to creep in.

What does this mean?

Where do we go from here?

"What now?" I ask. I turn my body toward him, propping my head with my hand.

"I don't know," he says.

My eyes wander down his chest and tour the place where I had sliced him with the scissors. The bruising isn't that bad anymore. It's starting to heal, but it will still take a while.

"I wanted to do that for a long time," Tyler says, turning his head toward me.

"Really? You wanted to sleep with me in the seventh grade?" I smile.

"I wanted to kiss you since the seventh grade." He laughs, shaking his head.

"I wanted to kiss you, too. I can't believe that we never did that before. Kiss," I clarify.

I blush a little and my cheeks get flushed.

"I can. You were my best friend and I was terrified of losing you. I wasn't sure you felt the same way and if I brought it up and you rejected me, I just couldn't imagine dealing with that."

"I wouldn't have rejected you. I had a crush on you the first time you stood up for me, back in music class. The closer we got as friends, the stronger my feelings got. I spent nights imagining what it would be like to actually kiss you and under what circumstances this impossibility could happen."

"Kids are funny, aren't they?"

I nod.

"But kids are really resilient, too," Tyler says. "I think back to all the shit that my dad did to all of us and I just don't know how I kept waking up in the morning and putting on a smile to go to school. I wore this mask for such a long time, this popular guy, this jock on the track team, this untouchable king of the school mask. Back home? I was terrified of my own shadow."

I slide my hand under the covers and find his. I intertwine my fingers with his and he squeezes me back.

"I'm really sorry," I whisper.

He looks at me as if he has been in a trance.

"Don't be. I'm over all of that. It happened in another life to another person and it has nothing to do with me anymore."

I give him a slight nod and force a smile, but deep down I know that can't possibly be true.

The scars we acquire as children stay with us our whole lives. Even if we are able to get past the pain and forgive, we never forget.

Every person who went through anything similar is a reminder of just how bad people can be.

ISABELLE

WHEN SHE TEXTS…

While we are still in bed, my phone dings and I see that I have a text from another one of my neighbors. Jackie lives a few doors down with her husband and son who is a little bit older than I am.

He's currently in the middle of a divorce and his wife has moved out. I remember her telling me about their custody battle and all the things that the daughter-in-law is trying to do to get more money and more time with her child, but I take that with a grain of salt. Divorces are complicated proceedings with lots of he said/she said details that often get lost when the grandmother relays the information to a neighbor.

Jackie and I have never been close, but we have never been particularly unfriendly either. It's just like with Pam. I tend to keep my distance and keep to myself, but her text takes me by surprise.

She is wondering if I could be a character witness for her son when this all goes to trial.

I don't really know your son very well, I text back. *I'm not really sure what I can offer the court.*

That's the thing, he doesn't have many people in his life that could stand up for him and tell them what a great person he is, but she's going to try to assassinate his character and he needs as many allies as possible.

I read the text twice, getting more annoyed the second time. She had completely ignored what I said, and just insisted on what she thinks she needs to happen.

I don't know your son well so I don't think it's a good idea for me to say anything about him in court. I wouldn't want to lie.

There's a long pause and she doesn't text back for a bit.

The thing about texting is that, on one hand, it seems like so much of an easier way to communicate, but it's not really the best for complex social situations.

In text, you are always missing the additional clues that give you some idea as to how you're being received.

Eye contact, facial expressions, body language.

There's nothing like that with texting, but I don't really care. I'm not going to be obligating myself to testify on anyone's behalf whom I don't know.

Okay, I understand, Jackie messages after I get up from bed and brush my teeth. *Do you want to sit down with him and get to know him a little better?*

I stare at the phone making a what the hell face in the mirror.

"What's wrong?" Tyler asks.

Unwilling to go into this anymore, I hand him the phone to read.

"She's got some balls on her," he says, raising his eyebrows.

I shake my head, annoyed.

"Wow, she really doesn't take no for an answer, does she?"

"I have spoken to this woman maybe a handful of times. Where the hell is this coming from? I told her I don't know her son so what kind of testimony can I even give? Besides, do they even take testimonies from random neighbors who have nothing to contribute to the discussion?"

He's about to say something, but I continue my rant.

"I mean, what am I going to say? That he's a nice person so therefore he should get his kid? Based solely on my two interactions with him when I saw him washing his car and he said hello to me at Starbucks?"

"Maybe, don't write *that* back," Tyler says, wrapping his arms around me from the back.

I'm wearing my bathrobe, but he is stark naked.

He starts to tug at the collar and then reaches down and unties the belt. My bathrobe falls open before me and I look at him in the bathroom mirror kissing my neck. I arch my body toward his as he slowly touches his lips to my skin.

He's soft and deliberate, making his way up to the back of my ear. Moving my hair out of the way, he takes my earlobe in between his teeth and gives a little bite. He exhales ever so slowly and I hear a quiet rustling sound swishing by me.

"Maybe, don't answer her anymore," he suggests.

I smile and turn toward him, putting my lips on his. I open my mouth and welcome his tongue inside. It's delicate and yet forceful in just the right way. His hands make their way into my bathrobe, along my skin.

They pause briefly at the small of my back before cupping my butt cheeks. With one quick motion, he lifts me up onto the bathroom counter in that spot between the two Jack and Jill sinks.

I open my eyes and he presses his body close to mine as I intertwine my legs behind him. His hands cup my breasts and then so does his mouth. I bury my hands in his thick, luscious hair.

After sliding my bathrobe off my shoulders and kissing the top of each shoulder, I free my hands and grab onto his cock. It's hard and thick and he knows exactly what to do with it. I've run my fingers up and down and then over his thighs and up his perfect six pack. His frame is wiry and thin, but incredibly strong with all the muscles protruding with each breath.

I don't hear the doorbell at first, but he does. He looks up at me, his eyes meeting mine.

"Who is that?"

"I have no idea." I shake my head.

The doorbell rings again and again. The person's patience is growing thin. Then I hear a female voice.

I wrap myself up in the bathrobe and tell him to wait here.

Who could that be?

Why the fuck are they ringing my doorbell like *that*? Right before I get to the foyer, I feel my body tense up as a thought rushes through my mind.

What if it's not an annoying neighbor?

What if it's the police? That sounds like their knock - loud and impatient. I take a deep breath and try to steady myself. When I walk a few steps forward, I see her peering into the glass.

23

ISABELLE

"Hey, Jackie," I say.

She takes a step toward me as if she expects me to invite her in. I close the door a little bit and offer no such invitation.

"Listen, I just wanted to explain what's going on in more detail. It's a really big deal. He has to get custody. Otherwise he's going to have to pay her who knows how much every month."

No apology? I want to say for ringing my doorbell a million times.

"So, he only wants to get custody so that he doesn't have to pay her child support?" I ask.

She stares at me, taken aback by my comment.

"No, of course not. He loves his child. He wants to spend as much time with him as possible."

"Listen, I understand but I just don't know what you want me to do about it. I don't know him very well. We've spoken maybe a couple of times. That's it. He should probably get one of his friends to do this."

"His friends are all losers," she insists. "They don't have jobs. They don't own property. Most of them live with their mothers."

You mean sort of like your son, I want to say, but, again, I bite my tongue.

"I'm about to get into a bath," I say. "I wish I could help, but I really can't. I don't know him and I don't want to lie."

"Please," Jackie says, putting her foot in the doorway just as I was about to close it for good. "I really need your help. He doesn't have the money to pay the child support so he has to get custody."

I feel bad for her, but it makes me a little

bit upset that she would think that I would side with someone like that, someone who might only want custody so that he wouldn't have to pay support.

Before I can say anything again, she leans a little bit closer to me and looks in my face.

"Where did you get those slashes? The cuts around your face?"

I bring my fingers up to my face to try to cover up what I know is already visible.

"Actually, I fell into a bush," I say quickly.

The best lies are those closest to the truth. "I was cutting it and I dropped the sheers in the back by the window so I tried to get them out without much success."

"Are your gardeners not doing a good enough job?" she asks with a concerned look on her face.

I shake my head and say, "I just saw a little twig that was out of place and got it in my head to fix it and, of course, this is what happened."

I can't tell by the expression on her face whether or not she believes me, but I pray that she does. That's the only explanation that she's going to get.

"Okay, good," she says after a long pause, narrowing her eyes with suspicion. "I was just worried, you know with everything that's going on."

My heart speeds up and I feel my hand form into a fist in the pocket of my plush robe.

"What do you mean?" I ask.

"Well, you know, about the manhunt for the convicts. The murderers that are on the loose. They are saying that there's a really good chance that one of them is hiding out somewhere in this community."

I give her a nod and try to force the expression of concern from my face. Whatever I show her seems to do the trick because she keeps going without waiting for a response.

"I just can't believe that there's somebody like that in our midst. You know what I mean? He killed his wife, her unborn child, and her boyfriend. Just stabbed them. Then he got out. I mean, don't they have guards over there? It's supposed to be a maximum-security prison. No one is supposed to get out."

I swallow hard trying not to say anything in his defense. It's better for me if I don't.

I'm not going to change her mind and I'll probably just make her more suspicious, which is the last thing that Tyler needs.

But I can't keep my mouth shut.

"Actually, I heard that he was long gone from here. I read that he's headed somewhere west. Arizona, Colorado, I'm not sure."

"Really? Where did you read that? I've been scouring Twitter and all the blogs and all the newspaper articles and I haven't read anything like that."

Fuck, I said silently to myself. I shrug my shoulders.

"It's probably just a rumor. I saw it on social media somewhere."

I'm about to bid her farewell when she stops me again, putting her weight on her back foot instead of her front and crossing her arms across her Steelers jacket.

Then she asks, "Hey, didn't you go to

school with him? He would've been just around your age."

"Well, there were three runaways."

"Yes, I know, I know, but two of them were from Philadelphia or somewhere out east. He was the one who actually went to Fox Chapel Middle school."

A big knot forms in the back of my throat and I can't take a breath. My body tenses and when I try to move, nothing happens.

I don't know what to do.

Should I pretend not to know him at all or would that be too suspicious?

"You went there, right?" Jackie asks.

Now it feels like the real reason why she came here is to interrogate me about this.

24

ISABELLE

WHEN SHE SHOWS UP...

"Actually, yeah, he did go to my middle school but then I moved away to a different district. Honestly, I don't remember who he is. I wish I could, it would make for a much more interesting story."

"Yeah, it would," Jackie agrees. "But it's probably for the best. I mean, who the hell wants to know someone like that?"

Luckily, she doesn't linger much longer. Also, she doesn't bother asking me again about her son, relieving me from saying no one more time.

She finally leaves and I let out a deep

sigh of relief. When I get back to my bedroom, I see Tyler sitting there crestfallen.

"What's wrong?" I ask.

He shakes his head, looking down at the floor.

"I didn't realize how much danger I was putting you in," he says quietly. "The cops are closing in on me and it's only a matter of time. I was so selfish in coming here and getting you involved in all of this."

"No, you weren't. I'm really glad that you're here."

The words come out of my mouth before I realize what I'm saying, but I know that it's the truth.

"Before you showed up, my life had hit a standstill," I explain. "I just stopped living for a little bit. When you came back into my life, I was reminded of everything that I was missing out on."

Tyler shakes his head and I can already tell that he doesn't quite understand.

"You can get some excitement in your life by going out to a bar once in a while, meeting up with friends, going dancing," he says. "You don't need a convict to break into your house and put a knife to your throat to feel like life is worth living."

"That's not what I mean and you know it," I say, looking down at the floor. "When you first got here, I was scared. I wanted you to leave. I was regretting not living my life to the fullest because if I had died then, what would I have to show for it? Then things changed. I realized who you were and how much you meant to me. I remembered how close we were. You were my best friend. After we moved, I felt like I'd lost someone really important. I kept thinking about you through the years and I wanted to reach out, but something stopped me. It was probably fear."

"What am I going do?" Tyler asks, shrugging his shoulders. "How do I get out of this?"

I shake my head and whisper, "I have no idea."

"What if I surrender?" he asks. "You won't get in trouble. Maybe I can get my attorney to work out some deal."

I furrow my brows. "Surrender? Why would you want to do anything like that?

You just started serving your sentence and they're going to tack on a whole bunch of years for escaping and for kidnapping me. If you don't tell them about me, then they'll still hold you accountable for the escape."

"I just don't see a way out. I watched the news while you were out talking with your neighbor." He averts his eyes and his voice cracks. "They caught Lester and they killed him."

I take a deep breath and hold it in my mouth before exhaling.

So, this is what it has been about.

This is why he suddenly is so sad.

"I'm really sorry," I say, sitting down on the edge of the bed next to him.

"Lester was a really nice guy. I know that it sounds stupid, but he was. He killed his father when he was fifteen years old because he had beat him and raped him practically every day since he was eight. Lester had had enough and he lashed out, but the jury didn't want to believe him. Even if some of them did, they said that he did it in cold blood. He bought the gun that he had and he waited for his father to come home. That was the only way he could protect himself. He was a scrawny teen and his dad was tall and as big as a mountain. After all those years of torment, he couldn't put up with it anymore. The only way he knew he could save his own life was by killing his dad."

I don't know what to say so I just sit on the edge of the bed and listen.

"After that, Lester buried him in his backyard and lived off his dad's Social Security checks. It was six months before anyone noticed a thing. When people started to ask questions, he just told them that his dad was out driving his truck. His dad mainly kept to himself so they bought the story for a long time. Eventually, someone reported it. I don't know who exactly, but the cops got involved and they found out that it was Lester who was cashing the checks."

I look down at my hands and move my infinity ring from one finger to another.

"The prosecutor told the jury that Lester killed his dad to get those checks, but that wasn't true. He was in tenth grade. He had no way to pay for rent or food. He had cashed those checks hundreds of times before with his father's permission at Walmart. He didn't do anything wrong. That didn't stop them from giving him thirty years, throwing him into prison, and throwing away the key."

"So, he ran away with you?" I ask.

"Yes, when we cut through the walls, he was in an adjoining cell in between me and Mac. We had to let him know what we were doing if we wanted to get away with it. Lester was timid and shy and he liked to draw quietly in his cell instead of socializing with everyone on the block. A lot of men took advantage of him and I think he liked to lose himself in his drawings."

Tyler leans over and buries his head in his hands. When he looks back up, his eyes are misty.

"He's dead because of me," Tyler says quietly. "If I hadn't asked him to come, if I hadn't insisted on it, he would still be there. Safe… well, moderately safe."

"You didn't do this to him," I say over and over again even though I know that I have no idea what I'm talking about. "He wanted to be free and he was for a brief period of time."

"No, I shouldn't have gotten him involved. He was a juvenile when he went in so who knows what kind of changes they would've enacted in the future. Perhaps, he would've gotten out on parole. One of his appeals might've worked and someone out there with power might've realized that he was just a kid who had been fucked with his whole life and he did nothing wrong in protecting himself. The one thing that I will never forgive myself for, however, is getting him involved with this."

25

TYLER

WHEN I FIND OUT WHAT HAPPENED...

Isabelle doesn't understand the full grasp of what I'm going through.

How can she?

Lester was more than my partner. He was the closest friend I had in there. He was thirty when we took off and he'd spent as many years in prison as he had on the outside.

He had given up on getting out of there a long time ago and just resigned himself to living a life in there. He got his GED, his high school equivalency degree.

He started taking classes toward his associate degree eventually getting his Bachelor's. He liked geology so he took a few classes on rocks and he also educated himself about the law. In fact, right before we ran away, he started taking classes through an online law school.

He had helped a number of inmates do their appeals as a paralegal and he wanted to be of even more use as an attorney. I don't know if he would ever be allowed to sit the bar exam and get his license, but that didn't stop him from believing in himself.

The escape? That wasn't his idea.

It was mine.

I had spent only two years in there and they were the worst two years of my life. I couldn't come to terms with myself that this would be my life forever. Besides, I was always the type to look for angles and shortcuts. Only my schemes never got anyone killed before.

I look up and gaze deep into her eyes.

"He shouldn't have died," I say with tears welling up.

I am unable to stop one and it rolls down my cheek.

"This wasn't your fault," Isabelle insists, but I know better. "He wanted to get away as much as you wanted to. It just didn't work out."

I shake my head. "He was never cut out to be someone to do something like that. He wasn't cunning enough. He wasn't willing to do enough to stay hidden. I don't know if I am either, but the truth is that in my situation, if I want to stay out of prison for good, I will soon have to make a lot of hard choices."

Again, she isn't convinced.

I realize that I have to be a lot more direct.

"To get away from there, he needed a car. You have to know how to steal one or you have to take one. Not everyone will give their car up easily and I don't know if he was willing to use force."

A different expression forms on her face. It's like she doesn't believe me or doesn't want to understand what I'm saying.

"He needed money for gas and for food. Again, there were no options except to just take what you need."

She shakes her head.

"You don't believe me?" I ask, challenging her eyes with mine.

"No, there must be another way."

"There is if you have someone helping you, but the problem is that you don't know who to trust. There's a bounty on all of our heads. $100,000 reward for information leading to our arrest. There are not that many people in the world who would not take that money in exchange for returning a murderer or three to where they belong."

Suddenly, it hits her.

Isabelle's whole body shakes as she comes to this realization, and after a moment she can no longer meet my eyes.

"What are you saying exactly?" she asks. "What are you trying to tell me?"

"I don't know," I say, licking my lips.

They are chapped and cracked and my mouth is dry from thirst.

"I don't know," I say again with a long sigh. "I guess I'm trying to convince you to do what's right."

"That is what exactly? Turn you in? Collect the money? Live happily ever after?"

"You would be doing society a great service," I say nonchalantly.

I don't know exactly why I'm pushing her to do this.

Anyone else would've done it already. Perhaps, I'm feeling particularly masochistic.

Perhaps, I feel like I deserve to be punished for what happened to Lester.

In either case, I just don't really give a shit anymore.

She finds my eyes and kneels down before me. Opening my legs, she pulls her body close to mine, snuggling up against my chest.

"I'm really sorry for your loss," she whispers into my shoulder. "You can't give up. I'll help you."

"No." I shake my head. "You can't. You shouldn't."

"I don't care. I don't want you carjacking anyone and I don't want you hurting anyone. I'm going to help you get where you need to go and then I'll come back home."

I hadn't considered this before.

I never wanted to get her involved at all,

but I would be lying to say it didn't sound like a great idea.

The truth is that I doubt that I would get very far on my own.

I don't know where Mac is or how far he got or what he had to do to get there, but I worry that my fate would be more like Lester's without her help.

"So, what happened after you got out?" Isabelle asks with some apprehension.

"We separated," I say. "We decided that it would be better if we each took our own journey in case they caught one of us. That way if they found one of us, they wouldn't find all of us."

"Do you know where your other partner is? Do you know where Lester went?"

I shake my head. "That's the whole point," I explain. "None of us were supposed to know anything about the others' locations. That way we wouldn't be tempted to make a deal."

"That sounds like a good plan," Isabelle says with a nod.

"Yeah, except when Lester ran into trouble there wasn't anyone there to help him. There's a reason why working together is more productive than going at something all alone."

"I know that you have a lot of regrets about everything that has happened," she says, "but I want you to know that it was a good plan. If you had both gone with him, what could you have done? If the cops caught up with him, they would have caught up with all of you."

I look up at her.

I hesitate for a moment, wanting to spare her feelings, but she clearly doesn't get it, so I have to be more explicit.

"If I had brought Lester here, then…" I say quietly, "he would still be alive today."

She doesn't say anything in response and I don't either.

I wonder what she's thinking. It was a terrible decision for me to even come by myself and it would've been worse to bring someone else with me. Yet, I can't help but think that if Lester had come here with me, then he would still be alive.

"Did you consider that?" Isabelle asks.

I shake my shoulders, uncertain as to how to answer.

"I don't know," I finally say.

"Don't lie to me," she says.

"Okay, yes, I did. I wanted to have a chance of getting out of there. I thought that here, with you, I would."

"So, why aren't *they* here?"

"Mac suggested that we each go our separate ways. We didn't discuss our plans on the outside. They don't know anything about them. I thought that I would be running away into the unknown just like they did. If they had known…" I don't finish my sentence out loud.

"What?"

"If they had known that I had this other plan, that I was coming here, then they would have insisted on coming with me," I say quietly.

"You didn't want them to?" She raises her eyebrows.

I think about that for a moment and then shake my head no.

"Why not?"

"I thought that it would put you in danger."

"Why?"

"Not everyone who is in prison is the same. Some of us, no, let me correct that, most of us are guilty of the crimes that we were accused and convicted of. I wasn't. Lester? He should not have gotten that sentence."

"What about your other partner, Mac?"

"He became somewhat of a friend in prison, but he's a very dangerous man. I didn't want to bring him here."

I grab the remote and turn on the local news. After a brief weather break and a commercial for soap, the news segment begins. I turn up the volume.

We are the leading story. They show our mugshots and leave them on the screen the whole time.

"That's not a bad picture," Isabelle says, giving me a wink. I have something of a smoldering, sexy look in mine.

I roll my eyes, shaking my head. "A lot of women think so, too," I add, only half joking.

"Oh, is that so?" she asks.

"Let's just say, I wasn't in need of that much mail while I was on the inside."

She wants to know more so I go over the broad strokes.

"I've received a lot of letters from people on the outside. Mostly women, but quite a lot of men, too. Some of them wrote just to tell me that they know that I'm innocent. Others wrote to commiserate and to say that they knew why I had to do it. All of them wanted me to write them back."

"Did you?"

"I wrote back to some, yes. It's nice having something to read and write. It gets lonely in there."

"Why would they want to be pen pals with someone doing thirty to life?" Isabelle asks.

"Your guess is as good as mine, but the psychological analysis is probably that they've been hurt a lot so writing someone, and maybe even dating someone who is that inaccessible is appealing. It's not like they ever have to worry about what I'm like out there in the real world."

"Yeah," she says, looking up at the ceiling. "I guess there's a safety in that."

A news anchor comes on and goes into more detail about Lester McCandless. Apparently, he was caught stealing someone's car. He didn't kill the man driving and didn't even take his cell phone so as soon as he hijacked his car, the man called the cops. Eventually, they ran him off the road and shot him to death.

"Why didn't he take the phone?" she wonders.

I don't have an answer to that question. I don't know why Lester did any of the things he did.

Lester did things like that.

He aimed for the impossible.

That's probably why he was studying for a law degree he could never use.

Perhaps, he didn't want to take anything more than he needed.

Perhaps, he didn't give it another thought.

In any case, his decision had cost him his life.

"So, what are *you* going to do?" Isabelle

asks, sitting down next to me and taking my hand into hers.

"Have I moped around long enough to bore you?" I ask.

"No, it's not that. I'm just wondering."

"I don't know. A part of me wants to just turn myself in. I'm injured. I don't have a car. I don't have any money. I don't want to ask you for help. I don't want to steal anyone's car. I don't want anyone to get hurt."

She squeezes my hand a few times and looks at a large print of a Chagall painting across from her bed. It's framed in a modern white frame, but I remember it from when she was a kid.

"Didn't that used to have an ornate gold leaf frame around it?"

"Yes, that's how I got it at the thrift store. I remember I paid $75 for it, all the money that I ever had in the world. I never told my parents, of course. They would go nuts that I had spent so much, but it brought me so much joy over the years. Still does."

"What happened to the frame?" I ask.

"It didn't seem to go with the house. I

wanted something modern and fresh. So, I got it reframed. The frame is still somewhere in the garage."

"It's pretty and it really lights up the room."

"That painting is one of my favorites. I mean, you can't go wrong with a bride and groom and an enormous, human-size chicken and a goat playing the violin, right?"

"Sounds like heaven to me," I say with a smile.

"Okay," Isabelle says, giving me another strong squeeze around my palm, entertaining my fingers. "I'm going to help you."

I whip my head around and stare into her eyes.

"No," I say sternly. "You don't know what you're getting into."

"No, I don't and neither do you, but you're not going to get out of this alive without my help. I know it and you know it."

26

ISABELLE

WHEN I KISS HIM...

When I look over at Tyler, I can't help but want to help him.

I know that I probably shouldn't.

He glances up at me with his big blue eyes. They aren't bright blue, just a little gray around the edges giving them a surreal almost magical type of quality.

His skin is pale, but luminescent. There's a quality to him that I really like. He isn't bombastic and overwhelming, but calm and reserved.

He's mysterious in every meaning of the word and it leaves me wanting more. I look up at him.

The tip of his tongue runs along his lower lip, adding a shine of gloss.

I close my eyes and kiss him. His mouth welcomes mine. There's no surprise now, like there was the first time we kissed. He doesn't need to ask permission and neither do I.

I don't know whose body collapses first, but we somehow end up on the floor. We make out for a while and I feel like a teenager again.

We're still wearing clothes but our bodies intertwine with each other's. Ten minutes later, it's not enough. This needs to become something more than a PG-13 movie.

I sit up for a moment and pull my shirt and bra off with one quick move. Whatever shyness I felt earlier, disappears.

As much as I don't particularly like my body, I can see it in his eyes that he does. He wants me just the way I am and there's nothing sexier than that. When he hesitates to take off his shirt, I quickly reach for it and pull it off.

He laughs as it gets stuck on top of his head. His stomach muscles flex and the parts that are damaged form delineated little muscles that make my mouth water even more.

I lean over and kiss his belly button and then around the V leading down to his cock. Tyler buries his hands in my hair, tugging slightly, just enough to send those bumps down my spinal column.

He runs his fingers up and down my shoulders and when I lift my body back up, he cups my breasts. Then he flips me over and cradles my head with his strong powerful arms. He helps me out of my leggings and I pull off his pants. We let our bodies touch and shivers run down my spine.

"I had dreamt of doing this ever since we were twelve," he says.

"That sounds… Not that great," I say with a laugh.

He laughs as well. "Hey, I was also twelve, remember?"

"You wanted to have sex with me then?"

"No, I don't think so. I just imagined what you would be like naked and what it would be like to kiss you everywhere. Mainly what it would be like to just have permission to look at you."

"I felt the same way," I say, my cheeks getting flushed. "If you had kissed me back…that would've been heaven."

"I was madly in love with you," Tyler says, the word love catches me off guard.

I haven't thought about that love in a long time, but the truth is that I was madly in love with him as well.

The problem was that we were both too afraid to say it.

Luckily, he doesn't wait for me to respond and instead kisses me again, and again, and again. He runs his hands over every curve on my body including the small of my back, the outline of my hips, and my nonexistent panty line. He's teasing me and I like it.

I want more. This isn't enough. He feels the same way.

I lie on my side and he drops his body over mine. I hear the rustling of a wrapper and a latex sound snap. A few moments later, he comes inside of me. It feels nice to lie on my side, my body smushed a little under his.

I put my arm over my head, arching my

back. He cups one of my breasts as he pulls in and out of me, slowly at first and then quickly gaining speed.

A familiar warming sensation starts to grow somewhere in my fingertips and my toes. It's a slow build at first and then in one moment it completely overwhelms me. I climax so quickly, it takes me completely by surprise as I gasp for breath. A few moments later, I feel him thrust into me faster and faster before eventually moaning my name into my ear.

———

As I GLANCE over at Tyler, asleep next to me, I feel at peace for the first time in a long time. This weekend has somehow showed me that I am more than the sum of my fears.

Life can't be defined by all the things I'm afraid to do. I wouldn't say that I have forgotten about my fears, or that they have completely evaporated during this time with him, but I would say that it has been a treat to not worry about every single human interaction that I encounter.

I don't know how to explain it exactly but having him here, in my house, puts me at ease. Tyler forced himself into my life and for that, I could not be more grateful.

But another fear sweeps over me.

What if I lose him?

It wasn't until he told me about his friend, Lester, that it has become somewhat of a reality.

What if the same fate awaits him?

Tyler is right.

He doesn't have any money and he doesn't have a car. To get either of those things, he will need to use force.

Unless I help him.

I hadn't planned on telling him that I want to help. The words just sort of came out of my mouth, but now thinking about it, I know that it's the right thing to do.

There are consequences that come with this decision though.

What happens if I get caught?

There's a manhunt for him.

Police officers and FBI agents and

federal marshals are looking for him everywhere.

What are the chances of us actually getting away with it?

But if we don't, then what?

If I'm caught helping an escaped convict, what becomes of *me*? They'll come after me.

I don't know the answers to any of these questions, but as I lie here twisting my ring in a circle around my finger, I look at Tyler's sleeping body and I know that I can't *not* help. Whatever the consequences may be to me, I have to give it a real shot.

I take a deep breath, shutting my eyes. I try to force myself to go to sleep.

We haven't talked about our plans or the future, but I know that whatever happens will be on my shoulders and it will be up to me to make it happen.

So, I need my rest.

I lie quietly for a long time trying to make my thoughts go away, but they don't. They continue to plague me. One stream of consciousness forms into another and then another and I keep going around in

circles until I feel dizzy and sick to my
stomach.

Unable to sleep, I pick up my phone,
unplug it from the charging cable, and turn
to one side, away from Tyler.

I check my emails, delete all the spam,
and venture over to Wayfair to look at the
sales on furniture and other home decor.
They have sales practically every other week,
but their emails always get to me and I can't
stop myself from clicking on the latest
discount.

Burying myself deep in different types of
patio furniture and decorative pillows, at
first, I don't see the text notification that
pops up at the top. I swipe up to make it go
away and only return to it later after I close
the page.

My heart sinks.

I read the text over and over again as my
hands turn to ice underneath the covers.

"Oh my God, oh my God, oh my God,"
I repeat silently to myself over and over
again.

27

ISABELLE

WHEN I GET THE MESSAGES...

Whatever sense of discomfort I felt earlier, trying to convince Tyler to let me help him, explodes and becomes a nauseating ball in the pit of my stomach.

Suddenly, I'm faced with the fact that my reason for wanting to help Tyler is not entirely altruistic. It's not that I have lied about anything, it's that I haven't been entirely truthful.

I read the messages over and over again without writing anything back.

I quickly delete them as well.

There will be more to come along with

emails and calls, but I will do what I can for now to keep a safe distance away.

After getting those messages, I am certain that I will not be able to fall asleep. Instead I head to the kitchen and make myself some comfort food.

I have a vegan cheese made from cashew in the refrigerator, which tastes identical to mozzarella. I grab some whole-grain bread from the pantry and make a big grilled cheese sandwich. I haven't had real cheese for a long time.

I was a fan a long time ago, but when I ditched meat and dairy, I obviously gave up cheese as well. Then, a few months ago, I bought this cheese alternative on a whim from Trader Joe's and haven't looked back since.

I know that if I ever want to lose weight then I should avoid bread and other things like that. I have been mostly good about it, but tonight is an exception.

I flip a grilled cheese sandwich on the pan and watch as little bits of it bubble and brown over the edge of the bread. My

mouth literally waters with anticipation.
After removing it and placing it on the plate,
I barely wait for it to cool down before
taking a bite.

Food has always been a comfort to me in
times of stress. There was a time when I had
control over it and I managed to get down to
around one hundred and twenty pounds. I
stayed there but not without great difficulty
and obsessive tracking.

Recently, however, I have let myself go. I
hate that expression. It's not completely true.

I know that people will say that it just has
to do with your calories in or the number of
carbohydrates you consume in a day, but I
have found that my ability to limit my
calories and limit my sugar is entirely
dependent on my level of confidence and
well-being. Also, being a lower weight has
given me some satisfaction when I look in
the mirror, but it hasn't always resulted in a
better quality of life.

There were times when I weighed the
least, but I felt and saw myself as the fattest
and ugliest. Fattest, it's often synonymous

with ugliest in our culture. That's the wrong kind of thinking, but unfortunately when I'm not feeling good about myself, I'm not immune to that kind of thinking.

I know that it's wrong. I know that I need to love my body because it's the only way forward. I know that I need to appreciate my body for everything that it does, because it does keep me alive and it does make me healthy.

Yet still, I can't help but judge myself based on the reflection that I see in the mirror.

I know that it's just a reflection, but that perception interferes with how I'm able to function in the world.

After consuming the sandwich in less than four bites, I stare at the empty plate, hating myself for what I have done. I should have taken my time.

I should have at least sat down and enjoyed every moment. The problem is that I can't really do that when my whole purpose for eating is to make these awful feelings about my body and my life go away.

My phone dings again and it's another

text from that number. I read it quickly and turn it off. I don't reply anymore and I shouldn't have even read them in the first place.

Yet curiosity always gets the best of me. I can't help but open them. I click off the phone and stare at my empty plate. It's as if I am suddenly infused with power, but when I flip the phone back on, I do something that I have never done before.

I block the number completely. I know that I should've done this months ago, but I never had the strength. There is always a reason to keep it unblocked. There was always a reason to maintain a line of communication.

I pour some water into the teapot and watch it boil. By the time I make a cup of tea, dunking the bag over and over again and watch it float up through the water, I realize that it's not the sandwich that gave me the strength to block that number. It's the man lying in the other room.

SITTING at my kitchen table and looking out at the darkness of my backyard, I focus my thoughts on solving the problem at hand. I had promised Tyler that I would help him, but he seemed reluctant to accept that.

The only way that he would say yes is if I came up with a sound plan.

What is that exactly?

I'm tempted to look up something on the computer, but I'm also terrified of the police going through my Google search results.

No, I will only do that if absolutely necessary.

In the meantime, I will just try to think of a good plan using the resources that I have; my own mind.

Feeling confined at the table, I get up and start pacing around my kitchen. I have never understood why walking and thinking seem to go hand-in-hand on television, representing a person who is deep in thought, completely focused on reaching some sort of impossible decision.

I hate to admit it, but it somehow fuels my thought process.

Maybe it has something to do with the motion of propelling yourself forward.

Maybe it has something to do with simply losing yourself in a stroll that allows your thoughts to stream freely. In any case, it allows me to focus on exactly what Tyler needs from me in order to get away.

The two main things that he had mentioned are money and a vehicle. Really, it's just money.

With money, you can buy a vehicle, even an unregistered one or is it one without a VIN number?

I can't quite remember.

I have watched hours of crime television shows and suddenly I don't know whether he needs a car that's registered to someone else or a car without any identification whatsoever.

"Ha. You thought that all of those hours were for nothing." I laugh to myself.

Anyway, he needs money.

I have some money saved up.

$7,000 to be exact.

I have that in my savings account and, if

I'm absolutely pressed for it, I have an additional credit limit on my credit cards.

One option is that I can take out the money from my savings account and just give it to him. He can then use it to get a car.

The problem with that is that by now, his name and face has been all over the news long enough for everyone in this area, and probably a few states over, to recognize him.

From what I've seen, they're even going to feature their case on America's Most Wanted next Friday. That show is shown all over the US and in a number of other countries. If he were to try to get a car himself, then the person selling it would inevitably turn him in for the reward money.

"Okay," I say out loud, my thoughts finally stabilizing. "What if we use my car?"

I can take some time off work, say that I need a break. We can use the car and drive out west, but what then? How long can I stay away without my coworkers and my neighbors suspecting something? They all know that I am a homebody, so it would be a big deal if I were to suddenly disappear.

If I do disappear and we take my car, then the police will have all of the information they need to find us. If they suspect that I have been kidnapped, then they will put out an All-Points Bulletin, telling all of the other police officers in all the states to look out for my car.

After pacing around the kitchen, the living room, and the dining room, I venture into the guest room. The closet doors are open from where Tyler used to change out of his prison clothes and into the sweats that my ex-boyfriend left behind. I'm not sure why I never threw them away when I got rid of practically everything else that belonged to him, but now I am thankful that I had kept them.

I keep pacing, walking slowly from the window all the way past the mirrored closet, into the bathroom turning around by the sink. Looking out of the smaller bathroom window at the neighbor's house, I analyze my options for how to make all of this work. Finally, I reach the only conclusion that seems feasible.

We will need another car. It will have to

be untraceable and, ideally, it should be registered to someone else.

Since it takes a bit for the car registration to go through with the state, I can theoretically still register it in my name, making it very hard for the authorities to track.

28

ISABELLE

WHEN WE MAKE A PLAN...

When Tyler wakes up, I start to tell him about my plan, but he quickly cuts me off.

"No, absolutely not."

"What are you talking about?" I ask.

"You're not getting involved in this. I'm not taking you on the run with me."

"I'm your only chance," I say. "What other choice do you have?"

He glares at me, his eyes focused entirely on mine.

"It doesn't matter," he says after a long pause.

"Exactly, you don't have any choice."

"I'm not putting your life in danger to save my own."

I shake my head. I feel my nostrils flaring up with anger.

"You already did, don't you see that?"

"I know and I feel terrible about it," he says, shaking his head. "You don't think that I do? You don't think that I regret coming here every moment that we're together?"

I look down at my feet.

One of them taps nervously on the floor, almost without my consent.

Does he really regret coming here?

How could he say that to me? I feel tears welling up in the back of my eyes. There is a profound sadness that suddenly sweeps over everything that I am.

Before he came here, I felt like I was moving through molasses. My life was one long pause after another. Then suddenly, he showed up and all of these uncertainties that have plagued me for so long started to disappear. They are not completely gone, they are still under the surface, like monsters under the bed, but it is daytime now and I'm not afraid.

"You regret coming here?" I ask.

"Yes, of course," he says with a self-assured shrug.

I turn away from him and start to sob. He takes a step toward me and wraps his arms around my body.

"That's not what I meant," he whispers into my ear over and over again.

I shake my head and wipe away the tears, but I still can't erase the pain.

"I don't regret seeing you again," Tyler says, spinning me around in his arms.

He takes a strand of my hair and moves it out of my eyes, tucking it gently behind my ear.

"Every moment that we spend together, I regret ever coming here because I find myself falling deeper and deeper in love with you."

When I hear that word, I look up at him.

I can barely see him through the moisture in my eyes. I blink and a tear falls down my face.

I watch him watch the tear travel all the way to my chin before taking his thumb and wiping it gently away. This is the first time that he has ever said *that* to me.

I haven't thought about it until this moment. I hadn't given the status of our relationship, if you could even call it that, any thought whatsoever, but love?

Of course.

Of course, I love him.

"I love you, too," I whisper softly, each word feeling like a cloud in my mouth.

"I didn't say it for you to say it back," Tyler says, holding me by my shoulders. "I just wanted you to know the truth about where I am. I told you that I didn't know why I came here and that was a lie. Maybe not at the time, but now I know that it was. I think part of me has always known that my heart belongs with yours. You were my best friend then and you are my best friend now. Only, I should have never put your life at risk by coming here. If only I had known this sooner…"

"I'm glad you came here, Tyler."

He lets go of my shoulders, exasperated, and sits down on the edge of the bed. He's dressed in nothing but boxer shorts and his wounds are healing nicely, but they are likely going to leave scars, a constant reminder of what I did.

Tyler puts his hands through his hair, burying his head in them.

"You have to *help me* help you," I say, putting my arm around him. "You might've come here for selfish reasons, but you actually have no idea what you brought into my life. I felt like I had been treading water for a really long time and then suddenly, here you are, and all of these pieces of the puzzle are starting to make sense."

I know that my words are cryptic, I don't mean for them to be, but I'm not ready to tell him everything about my past, not yet.

That's why he doesn't know that right now I need him as much as he needs me.

If I stay here much longer… things might get worse.

"I know that I don't have many options, but I just don't want you to be an accessory to my escape. If they catch you, if they catch us, they'll make you pay for it. It'll probably be a prison term. Unless…"

I look up at him.

The last word comes out as an afterthought, as if it is something that occurs to him at the end.

"Unless what?" I ask.

"Unless we make a backup plan. Yes, I think this is the only way this will work."

He looks up at me, his eyes shining brightly with the light bulb on the idea in them.

"You're scaring me," I say quietly.

"You have to promise me that if we get caught, you tell them that I took you hostage. You tell them that I made you do all of those things that we have to do to get away."

I think about that for a moment. "Won't that add a lot more time to your sentence?"

"I already have life. They will likely put me into level six, maximum-security, twenty-three hours in isolation, but I'm probably going to get that anyway. That is, if I survive."

"What are you talking about?" I ask, shaking my head in disbelief.

"Isabelle, people like me don't make it back. Cops all across the country kill people for a lot less. They're going to assume that I'm armed and dangerous. So, if anyone pulls us over or if anyone comes in contact with us, they're going to shoot to kill."

My body starts to shake as it dawns on me. Somehow, even when he told me about what happened to Lester, it never occurred to me that Tyler might actually be killed.

What kind of world would it be, what kind of life would I have, if he weren't on this earth drawing breath?

I start to shake my head so much that he actually puts his hands around my arms and pulls me close to him.

He wraps his body around mine and whispers into my ear, "It's all going to be okay."

"What if it's not?"

"It doesn't matter," he says, pulling away slightly to look at me. "Don't think about that. We don't know what's going to happen. Maybe it's all going to work out."

It seems like just a few moments ago, I was the one who was optimistic and positive and now the tables have turned.

"That's why you have to promise me,"

he says. "You have to promise me that if they catch us, you tell them that it's all my fault. I made you do it, but you didn't want to help me, not one bit."

"Okay," I say quietly.

"You have to promise me," he insists. "Actually say it. If they don't believe you, Isabelle, then this is all over."

"Okay," I say, my voice a little bit stronger and more self-assured. "I promise you, but in return you have to promise me something, too."

"What?"

"You have to promise me that you want things like that. If you promise me that you believe that this will work out and that you'll get away. The only way that this has a chance of working is if you believe in it."

He thinks about my proposition for a moment and then gives me a slight nod.

"I promise," he says.

I let out a sigh of relief.

29

ISABELLE

WHEN WE GET ANOTHER INTERRUPTION...

Afterward, we talk about the plan. At first, he wants me to just give him the money that I have saved, or rather a portion of it, as a loan, still fighting me on taking my help.

After a little while, he finally caves and agrees to let me buy him a car.

"You can't go by yourself," I say strongly. "Everyone has seen your face. You know this. Whoever you would buy the car from, would inevitably turn you in."

I feel like we've been over this before. I feel like we're going in circles, but I will continue to talk about this until he agrees to my plan.

He starts to say something about hitchhiking, but I cut him off immediately.

"I'm going to buy the car. I'm going to pay cash. I'm going to register it under my name and it will take a while for the registration and all that paperwork to go through. That way if anyone does suspect or even look for me, they won't know the year or the make of the car that we are driving."

Tyler shakes his head from side to side, unwilling to let me win, but we both know the decision has been made.

There are no other options.

This is the only thing that will work.

"I just don't want to inconvenience you so much. What if we just take your car? You can tell your coworkers that you're taking a trip."

"Yeah, I could, if I were the type of person who would just take a trip. I mean, that's what I'm going to say to them. I hope they believe me. I'll send pictures and proof of all the fun that I'm having on my travels, but the thing is that if they suspect that anything is wrong and if they go to the police, they'll know exactly what kind of car that we're driving. We need to be more careful. We need another level of separation between us and the authorities."

After getting dressed in the same sweats that he has been wearing all weekend, I also make a mental note that he will need some clothes; something suitable for traveling. Maybe even a new look.

"Have you given any thought to where you want to go?" I ask. "Let's say I get the car and we are actually able to get there. What then?"

"I don't know," Tyler says, walking past me out of the master bedroom and into the living room. Then, as if it has just occurred to him, he looks back around and looks at me.

"You're not staying with me, Isabelle. You're not taking me anywhere. I'll let you buy me a car and lend me money, but that's it."

A flash of anger rises from the pit of my stomach.

"Let me?" I ask in an incensed tone. "You will let me buy you a car and you will let me loan you money? Who the fuck do you think you are?"

I ball my hand into a fist, surprised by my own rage. It's not that I haven't felt it before, it has just never come out like this. Usually, I'm a very calm and deliberate person.

When he doesn't say anything in response, I throw my hands up and say, "Okay. I'm done."

I'm so frustrated by his arrogance and so-called protectiveness that I can't stand to be in this house much longer. I head to the entryway closet, grab a pair of sneakers, and walk out the front door.

My exit is so fast that it catches me by surprise. I wait for him to follow me, but of course, he doesn't. I glance back only once and see him look at me through the window on the side of the front door.

He has his arms open wide and is mouthing, "What the fuck?" but of course I can't hear him. So, I just keep going.

I don't go on runs often, hardly ever. In fact, I can't remember the last time I even put on my sneakers, but this time I just take off.

I don't warm up. I don't take my earphones to drown the world away with music. My phone is in the side pocket of my leggings. It sags a little with each step so I pull it out and continue to trot while holding it in my hand.

I barely get to the end of the street before I slow down to something resembling a half jog.

My lungs burn as I struggle for breath, but it feels good to be outside. The sun is shining for once. It's not exactly warm, but not bone chillingly cold either.

A few neighbors wave to me and I nod back. I should do this more often, I decide, when all of this is over. I push myself harder and harder hoping that the pain in my chest will somehow make the pain in my heart go away.

I know that Tyler is just trying to protect me, but that's precisely what's making me run with all of this rage.

Doesn't he understand that I need this to happen?

Doesn't he understand that I'm not doing this just to save him, but also to save myself?

"Excuse me, ma'am!" I barely hear his voice at first.

"Ma'am!" he says a little louder.

I come to an abrupt stop where my feet stop moving but the top part of my body continues in motion forcing me to wind back around like a slinky.

The voice belongs to a police officer in his forties with salt and pepper hair, wearing a windbreaker.

"Excuse me, ma'am, would you mind if I asked you a few questions?"

I have no choice but to give him a slight nod as a huge knot forms in the pit of my stomach.

30

ISABELLE

WHEN I TALK TO THE COP...

I collect my thoughts as I buy some time, trying to catch my breath. Part of it is that I have been running too hard and a bigger part is that I feel like I'm hyperventilating.

What is he going to ask me?

Why is he even here?

Why the fuck did I go running?

The intersection is two streets away from my house and this is the main road into the subdivision. This area isn't particularly busy but I guess this is what Jackie was talking about when she said that the road was blocked off.

The cop introduces himself as Walter

McVay. He is here alone with his car and the road isn't exactly blocked off.

"I'm sure that you have heard about the convicts who escaped from the maximum-security prison not far from here," McVay says in a casual, friendly sort of manner that's undoubtably intended to put me at ease.

"Yes, it has been all over the news." Before he can say another thing, I ask, "Is that why you're here? Do you think he's in this neighborhood?"

I try to express as much surprise as possible, even some shock for good measure.

"Yes, we have a reason to suspect that one of them is hiding out around here."

"Here?" I gasp.

"Nearby. That's why we're stopping all the cars and talking to all the residents to make sure that you are all safe."

"Wow," I say and let out a long sigh as my heart rate starts to speed up. "I just can't believe that someone like that would be here. I mean, this is a really safe neighborhood. We are all homeowners here."

I hate the way that sentence comes out

of my mouth, but I've heard my neighbors say it enough. There's a stigma against people who rent and everyone in this development seems to be very pleased of the fact that we are all homeowners here, as if there is something deficient about being a renter.

I've always hated that perspective, it's bigotry and small mindedness, but if the cop knows the people on this street, then I want him to know that I'm one of them and that he has nothing to suspect about me.

When a car pulls up to the intersection, McVay puts his hand up to stop the driver.

"I'm sorry, would you mind waiting for a minute?" he asks, without waiting for my answer.

He asks the driver, a man I don't know, a few questions by leaning over the window and then lets him drive through. Wanting to get out of the situation as quickly as possible, I start to run in place as if I'm trying to keep my momentum going.

After apologizing and asking for my name again, he hands me a flyer with the word WANTED on it with big block blood red letters at the top.

The picture on the first page belongs to Tyler's partner and the one underneath is his. I glance at his mug shot for a moment, his tousled hair, his bloodshot eyes, and the big black circles under them. Despite all that, he is still incredibly handsome and has a boyish grin that reminds me of the kid I used to know back in middle school.

"Wasn't there a third guy?" I ask.

"Yes, there was, but he has been… Apprehended."

"Killed? Right?"

The words escape my lips before I can stop them. He tilts his head slightly to the side, as if examining me with suspicion.

"I saw that on the news last night."

"He is a very dangerous person, ma'am, and we couldn't take him into custody like we usually do with suspects."

Feeling that he is suddenly on his back foot, I make amends.

"No, I didn't mean anything by it. I was just curious. I heard that he had been killed and I thought that maybe that was a mistake."

This seems to put him at ease and I even see him let out a slight laugh.

"Well, the news does tend to get some things wrong, but in this case, I was just trying to be more… Diplomatic."

"I understand." I let out a quiet sigh of relief.

I'm about to turn away from him and run when he stops me again.

"So, you haven't seen either of them anywhere around here?"

"No, not at all."

"Not on your runs? Not when you're just driving to work or to run errands?"

"No." I shake my head again.

"You haven't seen anyone suspicious? Maybe someone whose face you couldn't quite make out? Maybe someone in a jumpsuit or unusual clothing that stood out to you?"

"No," I say quickly, a little bit too quickly.

"I'd really like you to think about it for a

moment, if you can. This is really important."

"Yes, I know," I say, getting a little bit angry.

I don't like the tone of his voice, talking down to me as if I'm an idiot, but I have to play it cool.

"I haven't seen anyone," I say with a casual shrug.

"Well, in case you do, please don't hesitate to call," McVay says, handing me his business card.

I glance down at its glossy finish and then quickly tuck it into my side pocket where my phone used to be.

I give him a brief wave goodbye and take off.

31

ISABELLE

WHEN I RUN BACK...

I should head straight home, but I don't. Instead, I continue to run, or rather jog, for another mile.

My lungs start to burn and my whole body feels like it's on fire but I keep pushing myself forward.

I can't come straight back because the only way through is past a cop again and this has to be a legitimate jog.

Also, there's something else keeping me away.

I'm not ready to talk to Tyler yet.

I know that he doesn't want me to go along with him and I know that he thinks that I'm doing this purely for altruistic reasons. Perhaps it is time to tell him the truth.

The only problem is that if I do tell him the truth, then he might not let me come along at all.

The flyers that the cop handed me are bulky, even when they are folded up in quarters. When I stop at the end of the street, at the stop sign and wait for traffic to pass, I pull them out again.

At the top, right under the word WANTED, there's a line with the reward: $100,000.

"That's a lot of money," I say to myself.

Actually, it just so happens to be the exact amount of money that I need to get out of this particular predicament.

One hundred grand is going to make the texts stop coming.

No more anonymous calls.

No more threats about what's going to happen if I don't pay.

No more worries or fear.

I fold the flyers up quickly to try to put the thought out of my mind.

No, I can't do that to him. Absolutely not.

After I've been running long enough to make it look like a real jog, I swing back around and wave to McVay again. Much to my dismay, he waves me over again.

"Shit," I curse to myself as I force a plastic smile on my face.

"I hate to bother you again, but I just want to reiterate how important it is that you really be on the lookout for anybody that is out of place here. These kind of criminals are usually seen by joggers or dog walkers. People who move around in the neighborhood. People who see something that's amiss. People from the community."

"Yes, I understand. I'll be on the lookout."

"Okay, good," he says.

I'm about to leave again, but something holds me here.

I know that he isn't done.

"You know the crimes that they have committed and have been convicted of, right?"

I shrug my shoulders. "Murder?"

"Tyler killed his wife, his best friend, and her unborn child. Stabbed them to death. His wife's boyfriend was his partner who took his business away from him and then took his family away from him. The only problem is that he didn't commit the crime in a fit of rage. He planned it. Executed it. It was cold-blooded murder. The fact that she was pregnant, possibly with his own child, that didn't stop him."

His words swallow me as if they were an avalanche. I find myself struggling to breathe.

I don't know why he's telling me this unless he suspects something. When he starts telling me about Mac's conviction, I stop listening. I have been so keen on trying to help Tyler and lost in my feelings for him, that I never really came to terms with the fact that he might actually have done what he had been accused of.

I mean, most people in prison are guilty, right?

We lose ourselves in stories about underdog lawyers freeing innocent clients who have been railroaded by the system. But the truth is a lot more complicated than that.

"Isabelle?" McVay touches my arm slightly and I recoil away from him. "I'm sorry. I didn't mean to startle you."

"No, I'm sorry," I say quickly. "Yes, I understand all of that and that's all very scary and disappointing, but I don't really know what this has to do with me."

"Nothing," he says, taking a step away from me. "Of course, nothing. Except that you live here and we suspect that he's hiding out somewhere nearby."

"He?" I ask. "Aren't there two of them?"

"Yes, but they have separated. I'm not sure which one would be here, but we suspect that it's Tyler. He's from this area. Went to Fox Chapel High School. Did you go there?"

The question is so casual and unassuming, yet it takes me completely by surprise. For a second, I'm tempted to lie, but I already told Pam the truth and I'm sure she told Jackie. I don't want to be caught in a lie.

"Actually, I went to Fox Chapel Middle

School, but not the high school. My parents moved away by then."

"Did you know him?" He continues the questioning.

"I knew of him," I tilt my head slightly to the side, "but it was a big middle school and I don't really remember."

I wait for another question, but it doesn't come. Instead, he just stares at me.

I want to ask him if he has been interrogating all the male drivers and runners around here as much as he has been questioning (and intimidating) me, but I don't want to escalate this conversation.

McVay already suspects something. That is something that I can't change, but I don't want to make it worse.

I promise to call him if I see anyone suspicious or have any suspicion about anything and he's forced to accept this. Finally, he lets me go.

32

TYLER

WHEN SHE GETS HOME…

She leaves angry, without saying a word. I want to follow her, but I can't.

She slams the door behind her and I only get a glimpse of her rage as she disappears down the street. I pace around the living room, trying to figure out what to do.

The smart thing to do would be to leave now, but go where and with what money?

I hate to admit it but her offer to help is getting more and more enticing with each moment. I know that Isabelle is eager to come with me, but I'm afraid of what will happen if she does.

The thing that I worry about is the bullets. The years that they will tack onto my sentence, I can take, but what happens when the cops use all their fire power against us?

It happened to Lester. Luckily, he didn't have his girlfriend along with him for the ride.

Isabelle is right about one thing, though. If this is going to work, then I have to think positive. I have to think about this the way I did when I was building my multi-million dollar empire.

Nothing was going to stop me.

I was going after it no matter what.

Lots of other people have tried and most have failed, yet I didn't give a shit about the statistics.

I knew that it would work for me and even if it didn't, I would land somewhere so high up that it would be miles and dollar bills from the place that I came from.

I decide to wait for her.

I know that she's not going to turn me in.

She's just angry at me and I can't blame her. I need her to come back so we can talk about it. I need her to tell me about her plan.

As I pace around the living room, I try to figure out my own plan. Luckily, she has some savings and that's more than enough for a reliable used car with a considerable amount left over.

Her plan to buy a used car under her name is a sound one, much better than me going out there and trying to buy my own car from a stranger. Then, once we drive far away from this place, I can get my money back.

With enough money, I'll be able to buy a new identity and a new life, and as long as no one recognizes me, I can actually vanish for good.

I know that Isabelle wants to help me with this, but I don't know if she wants to disappear with me forever and leave her old life behind as if she's going into the witness protection program.

Probably not.

It's wiser for me to do it myself, but that doesn't mean that I won't be able to pay back her loan and pay her handsomely for her help in getting me there.

My injuries, which have healed significantly, start to ache and I'm forced to sit down in the recliner.

Yes, I decide this is what we'll do. This is how we will get out of this mess.

Twenty minutes later, the front door squeaks and Isabelle comes in.

"The cops are right out there, two blocks away, asking about you," she says and my heart skips a beat.

I'm not sure what to do except to follow her to the back of the house.

"Are they coming here?" I ask.

She pops her head around and says, "No, of course not. What kind of question is that?"

"I don't know. We were just talking and then you took off."

"I don't want to fight. We've had too many fights already. We need to make a plan and we need to get out of here."

She picks up her phone and searches for used cars on Craigslist. After reading a few listings, we find a 2005 Honda Accord in silver. It's not a very popular car around here, but it is out west and that's where we're headed.

Isabelle texts the number on the advertisement and the person on the other end texts back almost immediately. He's located a ten-minute drive away so they decide to meet in forty-five minutes.

"I'll go by the bank and get the cash," she says. "I'm also going to stop and get you some clothes."

I'm about to protest and tell her that I don't need anything, but that's not true. All I have is my prison-issued sweats and whatever I found in her closet that used to belong to her ex. It would be nice to wear something respectable for a change.

We don't talk about what happened but I do make it a point to apologize. She seems to accept that and I let it go for now. Then, right before she leaves, her phone vibrates as she gets another text.

It's an unlisted number and as soon as she sees it, all the blood drains away from her face. Her skin turns an almost blueish, green color, despite her being still flushed from her run.

I can't make out what the text says by the notification and she quickly turns off her screen. Tucking the phone into her pocket, I see it vibrate and light up again as she's getting a call. She pulls it out, presses the ignore button, and puts it face down on the counter.

"Who is that?" I ask.

"Nobody. It doesn't matter."

"It must be somebody if that's your reaction," I say.

"It's none of your business," she snaps back at me.

Now it's my turn to pause. I don't know much about her life. Whoever is calling might not be my business except that if she's going to travel with me, then it is.

I'm in a very precarious situation and I don't have many options. I know that it's not safe for me out there and, if I want to make it through this, I have to eliminate as much risk as possible.

I follow her into the bedroom and wait for her as she changes her clothes. She leaves her phone on top of the chair along with the rest of her clothes and I take a quick glance inside. I've seen her press her code enough times to know that it is 3378 and after I push the numbers, I click on the text log.

All of the messages after the car guy have been erased.

33

ISABELLE

WHEN I GO TO GET THE CAR...

I know that I should feel nervous about buying this car, but I don't. I click on the address that Chris, the guy from Craigslist, gave me, into Google maps and I follow the soothing voice of the woman giving the directions. On the way over there, the only thing I can think of are the threatening messages that I had received.

I had blocked their calls a few times already, but they just keep calling from different numbers. They won't stop making demands and threats.

They won't stop until I pay.

It doesn't take me long to find the house.

The guy waiting is about my age, overweight, and with a jolly expression on his face. It's not until I get out that I realize why he looks so familiar.

"Isabelle? Isabelle Nesbit?" he asks in that familiar, fun loving way that got him to be voted the most popular kid at our middle school.

"Christian DeParmo?" I ask.

"Yes," he says, extending his hand. "I go by Chris now. Makes it easier to sell cars."

My palms get sweaty. My breathing speeds up. He had tormented me for three years.

"So, where do you sell cars?" I ask.

" Usually from my car dealership. Out on Route 34."

"This one?" I ask, wrapping my arms defensively around my shoulders.

He doesn't take the hint. Instead, he takes a step closer to me and a big smile spreads across his face.

Clearly, he doesn't remember what he did. Or maybe he just doesn't care.

I look around. I need to leave, but the car is right in front of me…waiting.

We talk for a bit. He discovers that we went to the same middle school, but he still doesn't remember who I am. I try to deflect his questions as much as I can but he's curious. When I tell him what I do for a living, he looks impressed, mentioning that he didn't even graduate from community college.

I quickly pivot the conversation back to the car. When it's time for a test drive, I hope that he will let me take the car out by myself but I'm not so lucky. Chris climbs in the seat next to me and continues to tell me about all of our old classmates and teachers, as if we are some kind of old friends.

I drive the car for almost two miles.

I take it on the highway.

I drive it down different streets.

I hate being in the car with him, but I have to make sure that it runs well.

I speed up as quickly as I can when I merge and I come to a quick stop.

I put the car through its paces because I know that it has a long trip ahead of her.

"So, why are you buying another car?"

Chris asks. "Yours is the newest model year, isn't it?"

He and I both know that it is.

"I'm looking for a backup one. I'm planning on doing some remodeling on the house and I need to haul some stuff."

"You want to haul stuff in a Honda Accord?" he asks.

Shit, I say to myself silently. Of course, he's right. An old Honda is a terrible car to use if you need it for construction. It has two doors and a small back seat.

"Well, I have a Prius now and I need something affordable that would have a little bit more cargo space."

He gives me a nod and a shrug.

"Hey, I'm not judging, but, since we go way back, I have to tell you that you can just rent a truck from Home Depot or even a car rental place whenever you need it instead."

"Thanks, but I think I'll buy a car instead."

Chris throws his arms up in the air as if to say that he didn't mean any offense.

Despite the age, the car runs surprisingly

well. The only thing is that the transmission feels a little loose but that's to be expected.

Now is the part that I dread: the price negotiation. I'm ready to go as high as $3,000, but I really don't want to go over that. The listing price is $3,500.

Just as I'm about to ask about it, Chris mentions Tyler.

"You know what happened to him, right? He got life in prison for killing his wife and her boyfriend. Now he has escaped. I've been talking to all my old friends and we're joking around that one of us must be hiding him somewhere since no one can find him."

"What makes you think that he's still here?"

"The cops have blocked off all the streets They're practically doing everything but checking cars for stowaways. Hey, you'd have plenty of room to hide him in this trunk!"

My blood runs cold.

"Yeah, right." I smile.

"Someone must be helping him."

"Yep, you figured it out. Tyler found my

address, broke into my house, and has been hiding out ever since."

Chris and I both burst out laughing.

He laughs and I laugh.

I don't know why but I just decide to go with it.

"You know, that's why I'm buying this car. We're going to drive to Mexico."

"Hey, you know what's funny?" Chris asks after a moment. "I used to be really jealous of that guy. I mean, he was a multi-millionaire. He made his whole fortune in his twenties from nothing. Well, not exactly from nothing. I mean, I guess his dad had some money and was pretty well-off, but the amount of money that he made was well beyond that. When I heard about his hedge fund, his insane apartment, and his enormous house in Key West and another one out in LA, I thought, dammit, he did it. He made something of his life. I was really envious."

"And now?" I ask.

"Nope, not so much," Chris says.

Shaking his head, he runs his fingers over the bald spot on the top of his head.

"Now, I know that I have nothing to be jealous of, no matter how much money he made. He must've had some serious problems for him to do what he did, killing those two people and his baby."

"He didn't even know about the baby," I say.

Chris turns to me and his eyes narrow. Suddenly, I realize that I had said too much.

"What do you know?" he asks.

"Nothing. I mean, I read some articles about him and that's what they said."

"That's what his defense attorney said," Chris says after a long pause, waving me off as if my opinion doesn't matter.

I let out a slight sigh of relief because I have just made a mistake but luckily, I haven't been caught in it.

"Defense attorneys will say anything to get their clients off. I've heard that story, too. He just happened to come home and they were already stabbed and dead. The first time he heard about the pregnancy and the affair was at the police station, right?"

I nod.

"Well, that's horse shit. You know it and I know it."

I shrug and focus my eyes on the road, his house is somewhere in the distance.

"Listen, I don't mean to be rude, but I know guys like that. He felt entitled. He married her before he had money and he was probably running around with every twenty-year-old that he came across. Then when she had an affair, he got mad. He couldn't stand that someone who should belong to him disrespected him that way."

"You seem to be speaking from experience," I say, parking in front of his house.

"Okay, you've got me there," he says, laughing, tossing his head back. "If you ask my wife about it, my first wife, that's the story that she would tell you. Let's just not say anything to my second wife."

I get out of the car feeling nauseated but forcing a pleasant expression on my face.

When it's finally time for us to negotiate a price, he offers to sell it to me for two grand flat, as a discount to an old friend.

I take it. I thank him profusely and

promise to go to his next barbecue. I wonder if he thinks that giving me a discount on a seventeen-year-old car is going to somehow make up for all of the torture that he put me through. Either that, or he doesn't even remember what he did.

34

ISABELLE

WHEN I COME HOME...

On the way home, I stop by T.J. Maxx to get Tyler some clothing. I pop into the bank and then grab a burner phone from Walmart. I've never used this kind of phone before but apparently, it's untraceable because you buy the minutes upfront and it's not registered in your name.

After dropping the stuff off in the garage, I order an Uber and pay the ten dollars for the drive back over to Chris's house. That's where I pick up the keys for my new car and sign all the paperwork, handing over the money. Chris seems pleased with the fact that I give him cash rather than a check. We leave on good terms, but I hope I never see him again.

I park the new car in the garage, leaving mine out on the driveway. When we leave tomorrow morning at dawn, I'm going to switch the cars out, but for now I don't want any of my neighbors remembering the make and model of the used one.

When I come into the house, Tyler is freshly showered and dressed in his new sweats. He's wearing a loose-fitting white tee that hangs perfectly over his broad shoulders. His hair is a little long, falling slightly in his eyes in that sexy way that hair tends to do on attractive guys. He has made me a dinner of cauliflower rice, asparagus, assorted veggies, and fried potatoes. It's topped with a unique combination of herbs and spices, making my taste buds come alive.

"I want to thank you for everything that you're doing for me," Tyler says.

"Well, this is delicious," I say, taking another gluttonous bite.

"There's more," he says, raising one eyebrow.

I glance up at him.

His blue gray eyes sparkle and the rays of the setting sun sprinkle over his skin.

"I'm going to do bad things to you tonight," he says. "I'm not going to take no for an answer."

I lick my lips, leaning back in my chair.

"Is that a promise?" I ask. "What do you have in mind?"

"It's a secret. You're going to have to wait and see."

"Now that sounds like a threat."

I want him to take me right here, right now. I want him to bury his hands in my hair, but instead, he teases me. He clears the table and offers me dessert. It's a key lime pie with fresh whipped cream, but when it comes time for me to take a bite, he shakes his head.

"No? What do you mean no?"

"You can't have any," he says, licking his lips and cutting his slice with his fork.

"Close your eyes," he commands.

I do as he says and I start to feel an unfamiliar tingling feeling somewhere in my extremities.

Tyler leans closer to me and I feel his

exhale on my skin. My whole body shivers with each breath.

"Open your mouth," he instructs.

I do as I'm told and he places something sweet and sour, but amazing on the tip of my tongue.

I'm tempted to open my eyes but he stops me.

"Do everything I say and I will thank you in a way that you have never been thanked before."

"Yes," I whisper.

"Open your mouth more."

I do and I feel a chill. Another explosion of taste hits me. It comes on something soft, a finger. I lick up every last bit of the crust and the crumbs and the key lime filling along with the whipped cream.

"I'm going to put a blindfold over your eyes," he whispers into my ear after he gives me a slight kiss on my lips.

My heartbeat quickens and I grab onto the chair for stability.

Something soft brushes over my eyes as he ties it behind my head.

Then he tells me to stand up.

"Take off your shirt," he whispers.

The tingling in my toes and fingers becomes more of a gnawing feeling in my core.

I do as instructed.

"Take off your pants."

I peel off my leggings as graciously as I can, which is to say not particularly. I almost trip and fall, but he catches me.

"Open your legs wide."

I take a step to one side and then the other until they're both shoulder width apart.

"I'm going to pull off your panties," he says.

My body shivers and I give him a nod.

He pulls them down gently and allows me to step out of them. Then he unclasps my bra. I feel my breasts fall open before him. They suddenly feel very heavy and bigger than they normally do.

I try to suck in my stomach, suddenly keenly aware of just how much I ate.

He whispers, "You're the most beautiful woman in the world."

My body relaxes all on its own.

Tyler takes my breast into his mouth. I feel the tightness of his lips around me and I clench my legs when the feeling of pleasure starts to overwhelm me.

"Sit down," he says and pushes me into the chair.

I hear the rustling of clothes and when I reach my fingers over to him, they run over his strong, hard abs.

When I let them drift further down, I don't encounter anything but skin.

"Open your mouth," he says.

I wait as he hesitates for a moment before pushing something hard and thick into it. Much to my surprise, it also tastes like heaven. He covered his cock in whipped cream and a few bits of key lime meringue.

I wrap my mouth around him and move my head up and down, licking every last bit. His hands are in my hair, pulling it up into a high ponytail. He sends shivers down my spine. Afterward, his hands make their way down to my breasts, cupping them both from the top. Tyler squeezes my nipples in between his fingers as I continue to move my mouth up and down his shaft.

He pulls away after a little while and I reach for the covering over my eyes, but he stops me, lightly slapping my hand away.

"We're not done here," he says.

I can hear the teasing tone in his voice. He likes playing games and I like to play games with him.

"Sit back," he says.

I lean my back against the chair.

"Open your legs."

Again, I do as he requests.

"Prop your legs up on the chair and keep them open," he demands, giving me a kiss on the lips.

Suddenly, I get very self-conscious.

This is the worst way to sit for my stomach. It's going to make a hundred different folds, but he insists.

"Please do as I say. You won't regret it."

I take a deep breath and pull my ankle up to one side of the chair and then the other to the opposite side.

Luckily, the chair is wide and spacious, a classic wing back, and there's plenty of room. I hear him get down on the floor and then I feel his tongue on me.

His fingers make their way around, activating every impulse and erotic sensation in my body.

When they make their way inside, I hold my head back and lose myself for a bit.

I feel so open and exposed and yet completely safe and loved. I don't think I'm perfect, but somehow in this moment *we* are.

Right before I feel myself reaching the end with that familiar wave coming over my whole body, he stops and pulls away.

"Wait," I whisper, frustrated and annoyed.

"We have the whole night ahead of us."

I let out a deep sigh.

I don't want the whole night.

I want him now and quickly.

I need him inside of me or I'll explode.

He helps me out of the chair and leads me to the bedroom. There, he puts me on all fours and then goes to the dresser and pulls out my vibrator.

"I found your little bag of tricks," he whispers coyly.

If I weren't in this exact position and we

were clothed having this conversation, I would probably be embarrassed.

Now? Not at all.

"Yeah, like you don't touch yourself," I say as confidently as possible.

"Of course I do. Everyone does. I'm not here to make you feel bad about anything. Actually, I like it. I want to watch you use it."

Suddenly, my heart stops.

"You want to watch me?" I shake my head.

"Come on," he urges me. "It's so sexy. A woman pleasuring herself. A woman in control of her own body? I love that. I want to see you use it."

I make a move to get it, but he turns it on and hands it to me. I'm still blindfolded, and that makes me even more aroused.

I open my legs wider and press the small vibrator to my clitoris. It's smooth and soft and moves at a very nice pace. On all fours, exposed, doing something that I have never done in front of another human being, is beyond arousing. I feel how wet I am and I know that I won't last much longer.

Sensing my urgency, Tyler reaches for

my hips and thrusts himself inside of me. With each move, he gets deeper and deeper as my body takes him in further.

One time, I almost lose my balance, propping myself up with only one hand, but he catches me and puts a pillow in front of my face in case I fall again.

As we continue to move as one, two bodies become completely in sync. It doesn't take me long.

I press the vibrator a little harder and then even move it up and down his cock. He moans into my ear. Then suddenly, I lose my balance and collapse, just as a big wave of pleasure rushes through everything in my body.

A few moments later, he collapses on top of me.

WE LEAVE EARLY the following morning. It's still pitch black outside when the alarm clock goes off on my phone.

We have everything packed and we just throw in a few essentials. Right before he gets into the trunk of the car, Tyler asks me one more time if this is something that I want to do. I nod yes and throw my purse into the front seat.

With my old car parked safely in my garage, I drive out under the blanket of the night. There's a police officer waiting at the intersection, but he doesn't stop me. I drive all the way to Ohio, a full hour away, before stopping in an alley and letting Tyler out of the trunk.

"That was really sexy last night," he says when we pull into the gas station nearby.

"Yes, it was," I agree.

"I have so many ideas of other things we can do," he says.

My heart skips a beat and I tap my left foot impatiently. I have never felt this way about anyone before.

It's not just that I love him.

I also want him on that cellular level that combusts between two people.

"Maybe tonight we can do something… Dangerous?" I ask.

"Like what?"

"I don't know," I say, shaking my head. "Maybe more of what we did last night?"

"Maybe take it a little further?" he asks. "Did you like being tied up?"

I nod.

I never thought that I would, but it felt so freeing. I gave up control and all of my worries and anxieties went away with them. It was like I was no longer responsible for what happened to me and that made me feel so much better.

"I want to do bad things to you," he says.

"I like the sound of it," I say.

I give him a slight kiss and ask him if he wants anything from the store inside.

He shakes his head no.

It's only twilight and with his collar pulled up and his hair lowered over his eyes, Tyler is impossible to recognize.

I grab my purse and blow him another kiss on the way inside the store. I don't know what's going to happen to us, but I know that being with him feels like the first right thing that I have done in a long time.

A few minutes later, I emerge with my

arms full of packets of pretzels, Skittles, and Gatorade and a big smile on my face. Finally, this road trip is going to begin.

But when I look around, I don't see either Tyler or my car.

They are both gone.

THANK you so much for reading THE PERFECT STRANGER!

I hope you are enjoying Tyler and Isabelle's story. Can't wait to find out what happens next? Their story continues in the next book.

Read THE PERFECT COVER now!

When Tyler McDermott escapes from prison, he takes me hostage.

No, I do not fall in love with my captor.

Tyler is an innocent man who was framed for a heinous double murder.

Of course, I do not know that yet.

All that I know is that he has a knife to

my throat. All that I know is that if I want to live, I have to let him in.

This simple act of courage will change my safe life forever and show me that true love is possible after all.

But what happens when that love is not enough?

Read THE PERFECT COVER now!

CAN'T WAIT and want to dive into another EPIC romance right away?

Read ALL THE LIES now!

To save my job, I have to get an interview with a reclusive bestselling author who is impossible to find.

It's an insurmountable task until I get a lead. It's probably a joke but given what just happened in my personal life, it's an excuse to get away.

The last person I expect to see there is ***him,* the dashing and mysterious**

stranger who was the only man who knew the truth *that* night.

He invites me inside under one condition: everything he says is off the record. He'll answers my questions but I can't write about him.

Then things get even more complicated.

Something happens between us.

His touch ignites a spark. His eyes make me weak at the knees.

We can't do this.

But then he looks at me in that way that no one has ever looked at me and I can't say no…

Read ALL THE LIES now!

CONNECT WITH CHARLOTTE BYRD

Sign up for my **newsletter** to find out when I have new books!

You can also join my Facebook group, **Charlotte Byrd's Reader Club**, for exclusive giveaways and sneak peaks of future books.

I appreciate you sharing my books and telling your friends about them. Reviews help readers find my books! Please leave a review on your favorite site.

Sign up for my newsletter: https://www.
subscribepage.com/byrdVIPList

Join my Facebook Group: https://www.
facebook.com/groups/276340079439433/

Bonus Points: Follow me on BookBub and
Goodreads!

ABOUT CHARLOTTE BYRD

Charlotte Byrd is the bestselling author of romantic suspense novels. She has sold over 600,000 books and has been translated into five languages.

She lives near Palm Springs, California with her husband, son, and a toy Australian Shepherd. Charlotte is addicted to books and Netflix and she loves hot weather and crystal blue water.

Write her here:

charlotte@charlotte-byrd.com

Check out her books here:

www.charlotte-byrd.com

Connect with her here:

www.facebook.com/charlottebyrdbooks

www.instagram.com/charlottebyrdbooks

www.twitter.com/byrdauthor

Want to hear about new releases, free books and get exclusive giveaways?

Sign up for my newsletter!

Sign up for my newsletter: https://www.subscribepage.com/byrdVIPList

Join my Facebook Group: https://www.facebook.com/groups/276340079439433/

Bonus Points: Follow me on BookBub and Goodreads!

 facebook.com/charlottebyrdbooks

 twitter.com/byrdauthor

 instagram.com/charlottebyrdbooks

 bookbub.com/profile/charlotte-byrd

ALSO BY CHARLOTTE BYRD

All books are available at ALL major retailers! If you can't find it, please email me at charlotte@charlotte-byrd.com

The Perfect Stranger Series
The Perfect Stranger
The Perfect Cover
The Perfect Lie
The Perfect Life
The Perfect Getaway
The Perfect Couple

All the Lies Series
All the Lies

All the Secrets
All the Doubts
All the Truths
All the Promises
All the Hopes

Tell me Series
Tell Me to Stop
Tell Me to Go
Tell Me to Stay
Tell Me to Run
Tell Me to Fight
Tell Me to Lie

Wedlocked Trilogy
Dangerous Engagement
Lethal Wedding
Fatal Wedding

Tangled Series
Tangled up in Ice
Tangled up in Pain
Tangled up in Lace
Tangled up in Hate
Tangled up in Love

Black Series
Black Edge

Black Rules

Black Bounds

Black Contract

Black Limit

Not into you Duet
Not into you

Still not into you

Lavish Trilogy
Lavish Lies

Lavish Betrayal

Lavish Obsession

Standalone Novels
Dressing Mr. Dalton

Debt

Offer

Unknown

Printed in Great Britain
by Amazon